Jake Drake
CLASS CLOWN

Jake Drake
CLASS CLOWN

ANDREW CLEMENTS

Contents

CHAPTER ONE

New Boss

I'm Jake, Jake Drake. I'm only ten years old, but I already have a full-time job. Because that's sort of how I think about school. It's my job.

I'm in fourth grade now, so I've had the same job for more than five years. And if you do something long enough, you get pretty good at it. That's how come I'm starting to be an expert about school.

I've had a bunch of different bosses so far. Because that's what a teacher is: the boss. And one thing I know for sure is that it's no fun when your boss is a sourpuss.

So far things have been okay for me. A few of my teachers have gotten grumpy now and then, and a couple of them have really yelled once in a while. And this year my fourth-grade teacher is Mr. Thompson, who can get grouchy sometimes. Plus he has brown hair growing out of his ears. So he might be a werewolf.

Still, I've never had a real sourpuss for a teacher—at least not for a whole school year.

But not Willie. Willie's my best friend, and last year his third-grade teacher was Mrs. Frule. She's one of those bosses who walks around with this mad look on her face, sort of like a cat when it's outside in the rain. If you go past her room, you feel like you should whisper and walk on tiptoe. Because if Mrs. Frule even looks at you, she can always find something to get mad about.

So third grade was tough for Willie because he's the kind of kid who loves to smile. Putting Mrs. Frule and Willie into the same classroom was a bad idea.

When I met Willie at lunch on our first day of third grade, I could tell something was wrong. He looked sort of pale, like maybe he was going to keel over or something. I said, "Hey, are you okay?"

And he said, "No, I'm *not* okay. Mrs. Frule already hates me. I spent half the morning getting yelled at, and the other half trying to figure out what I was doing wrong."

I asked, "What happened?"

Willie shrugged. "That's what I don't get. I

didn't *do* anything . I was just sitting there, and all of a sudden I saw Mrs. Frule looking at me. So I smiled at her, and she frowned and said, 'Young man, wipe that smile off your face.' So I did. I wiped my hand across my mouth like this, and I stopped smiling. But that mad Robbie Kenson start laughing, so then Mrs. Frule got real mad and she made me get up and walk out into the hall. And then she came out and leaned down, like, right into my face. She got so close I could see all the way up her nose. And she shook her finger at me and said, 'If you ever act like a smart aleck in my classroom again, you are going to be very, very sorry!' "

Poor guy. That was only Willie's first day of third grade, and it didn't get any better. All year long Mrs. Frule yelled at Willie at least three times a week. And he's one of the *good* kids!

The kids like Jay Karnes and Zack Walton—real troublemakers? For those guys, being in Mrs. Frule's class was sort of like being in a prison camp. Maybe worse, because in a prison camp, if you mess up, you don't have to get a note signed by your parents.

My third-grade teacher was Mrs. Snavin, and she was pretty nice most of the time. I wished Willie could have switched to my class. But it doesn't work that way. Once school starts, you're stuck with your teacher for the whole year, and you just have to make the best of it.

And that's what Willie did. He didn't have a lot of fun in third grade, but he lived through it. Even Jay and Zack survived. Because that's what you do when your teacher is a grumphead. You learn what you have to do to stay alive, and you do it. And you know that once the year is over, you'll never have that boss again. So you just do your best and wait for summer.

Like I said, most of my teachers have been pretty nice. Actually, the grumpiest teacher I've had so far wasn't even a teacher. She was a student teacher. And I didn't have her for that long. Only about three weeks. Which was plenty. Her name was Miss Bruce.

Miss Bruce showed up on a Monday morning in April near the end of second grade. Mrs. Brattle was my regular teacher that year, and she said, "This is Miss Bruce. She's in college, and she's studying to be a teacher. As part of her college work, she's going to be here in our classroom for a while."

I looked at Miss Bruce. She was younger than Mrs. Brattle. A lot younger. She was so young that she sort of looked like Link Baxter's big sister. Except Link's sister was only in high school. Plus part of her hair was colored pink. Or sometimes purple.

Miss Bruce's hair was reddish blond. That first day she had on a blue shirt and a green skirt and blue shoes. Her nose was kind of small. Or maybe her nose was mostly hidden, because she wore a big pair of glasses with black rims. And her nose had freckles, too.

For her first three days Miss Bruce didn't do much. Sometimes she helped Mrs. Brattle pass out papers. Once she read part of a story out loud. But most of the time she just sat in a chair near the back of the room and watched.

By Wednesday we'd gotten used to her hanging around. No one paid much attention to Miss Bruce. Except me. I kept looking at her during those first three days.

And I noticed something.

Back in second grade, Willie and I were both in Mrs. Brattle's class, so at lunch on Wednesday I asked Willie a question. I asked, "Have you noticed anything funny about Miss Bruce?"

"Funny?" said Willie. "You mean like the way she squints and wrinkles her nose when she looks at the chalkboard? I think that's kind of funny, don't you?"

"No," I said, "I mean funny like strange. Have you ever seen her smile?"

Willie was scraping the icing off an Oreo with his front teeth. He stopped right in the middle of the cookie. His eyes opened wide and he said, "You're right! I haven't seen her smile at all! Have you?"

I shook my head. "Nope. Not once. I wonder why."

Willie finished his first scrape and then started licking the leftovers. He stopped with his tongue sticking out. Then he gulped real fast and said, "Hey! Maybe she *can't* smile! Maybe she has a special problem, like if she smiles, her teeth fall out or something! Or maybe...maybe she's...an *alien!* Yeah, she's an alien, and she doesn't know how to smile, and...and she's going to use her special powers...to turn all of us into hamburgers and beam us up to her spaceship!"

Willie's like that. He has a lot of imagination.

But in a way, Willie was right. Miss Bruce *did* seem to have some special powers.

And there was one power she had that was going to change my life for a while. Because Miss Bruce was about to turn me into Jake Drake, Class Clown.

CHAPTER TWO

Scared Stiff

Thursday morning Mrs. Brattle asked us all to be quiet and listen. She asked Miss Bruce to come and stand next to her at the front of the classroom. Then Mrs. Brattle said, "For the next several weeks, Miss Bruce is going to be your teacher. I'm going to be helping Mrs. Reed in the library during this time, so I'll probably see you every day. And I'll even be here in the classroom sometimes. But Miss Bruce will be your teacher. I want all of you to be on your very best behavior for her."

And then Mrs. Brattle picked up her purse and a stack of papers and walked out of the room.

We all sat at our tables and looked at Miss Bruce. And Miss Bruce stood there at the front of the room and looked at us. Then she said, "Let's begin by talking about the rules." Her voice sounded kind of high and squeaky. "First of all, it is going to be quiet in my classroom. No talking, no whispering , and no shouting or laughing. You may not talk unless you raise your hand first and I give you permission. We have a lot of work to do, and we don't have time for any fooling around. I have very high expectations for each one of you, and I'm going to demand excellence. Is that clear?"

Miss Bruce lifted up her eyebrows, all the way above her big glasses. And she looked around the class. And she didn't smile.

I looked around too and I could see this look on everyone's face. Sort of a scared look. Even Link Baxter looked scared, and that almost never happened.

Then Miss Bruce clapped her hands together twice and said, "All right. Now. Let's not waste any time. Please get out your math workbooks."

Laura Pell raised her hand. When Miss Bruce nodded at her, Laura said, "We always have reading before math."

Miss Bruce didn't smile. She said, "What's your name?"

"Laura."

Miss Bruce said, "Laura, I want you to

answer a question for me, all right?"

In a real small voice Laura said, "Okay."

"Now, Laura," said Miss Bruce, "who is your teacher?"

Laura smiled, because that was an easy question. She said, "My teacher is Mrs. Brattle."

Miss Bruce raised her eyebrows and leaned forward, and she said, "Now, Laura, please think. What did Mrs. Brattle just say? Who is your teacher for the next few weeks?"

In a tiny little voice Laura said, "You are."

Miss Bruce nodded at her and said, "That's right, Laura, *I* am your teacher now. And what did I ask you to do a minute ago?"

Laura said, "You said to get out our math workbooks."

Miss Bruce nodded. "And now I'm going to say it again: Class, please get out your math

workbooks."

So we did. We all got out math workbooks. Then we turned to page 47 like Miss Bruce told us to, and we did some addition problems. There was no talking. There was no whispering. There was no looking out the window. And there was no smiling.

We took the worksheet out of the workbook when Miss Bruce told us to. We wrote our names on our papers when Miss Bruce told us to. Then we passed in the papers. Quietly.

Then it was time for social studies. We had to read three pages in our *People and Places* book. Quietly. And then answer some questions on page 83. We had to write down our answers with no talking and no looking at our neighbors' papers. That's what Miss Bruce said. Like she thought we might cheat. And she didn't smile.

I looked over at Laura Pell. Her face didn't move, sort of like she was wearing a mask. She sat up straight in her chair. She didn't smile at all. She kept her eyes looking down at her table. When she was done with her work, she folded her hands and put them in her lap. She looked like a statue.

And I knew why Laura was acting that way. She was scared of making a mistake. She was scared of Miss Bruce—scared stiff. Because when you get a grumphead for a boss, that can happen. And if your boss is grumpy and fussy and picky all at once, it's extra scary.

It was so quiet in our classroom. All I could hear was the squeaking of Miss Bruce's blue shoes as she walked around the room.

I took a quick look at the rest of the kids. Willie was scared. And Andrea Selton. Everyone was scared stiff, even Ben Grumson, who was even tougher to scare than Link Baxter.

And so was I. I sat still. Willie was sitting at my table, just two feet away, but I never looked at him. Because I was afraid we might smile at each other and get caught. And then Miss Bruce might get mad at us.

A part of me had decided to be careful. Part of me wanted to make sure there wasn't any trouble.

But there was another part of me that didn't want to sit there like a bag of potatoes. This other part of me didn't want to just fold my hands and look down at my desk.

There was a part of me that didn't care if Miss Bruce got mad. That was the part of me that wanted to stand on my head and stick out my tongue and yell, really loud.

But did I?

No. That first day when Miss Bruce took over our class, I didn't dare.

I was too scared, just like everyone else.

CHAPTER THREE

Scared Silly

I'm usually happy on Friday mornings.

Friday means that the next day is Saturday, and on most Saturdays Willie and I mess around together. We watch some TV. We ride our bikes, play some computer games, and mostly have fun. If the weather's good, we work on our fort in the woods behind Willie's house. So Friday means work is almost over for the week.

But the Friday after Miss Bruce took over, I didn't feel happy. It felt like it was going to be the hardest day of my life.

On the bus ride to school that day, I thought, *Maybe Miss Bruce will be nicer today. Maybe she'll smile a little. Today will probably be a lot better than yesterday.*

I was wrong.

Friday started off like Thursday had. First we did a math worksheet. Instead of passing them in, we exchanged papers. Miss Bruce read the right answers for us. And she never smiled.

Then we did a map-skills sheet for social studies. We marked North, South, East, and West. We colored the rivers and lakes blue. We found the railroads and the highways. We

found the mountains and the cities. Then Miss Bruce turned on the overhead projector and showed us how our maps should look. She said we could fix our maps if we had any mess-ups. That was sort of nice of her, but she never smiled.

Gym was great. Not because I love gym, because most of the time I don't. Gym was great because Miss Bruce wasn't there.

After gym, we all went back to class. There was no laughing, and nobody was late, not even on second.

Then Miss Bruce said we were going to have a spelling bee, and everyone was glad. Spelling bees are always fun, right? Wrong. Not when Miss Bruce is the boss.

Miss Bruce looked down at the seating chart and then looked through her big glasses at Meaghan Wright. She said, "You'll be first, Meaghan. Remember the rules: You have to say the word, then spell it, and then say it again. Ready?"

Meaghan nodded, so Miss Bruce said, "The first word is 'mouse.'"

Meaghan looked up at the ceiling. Then she took a deep breath and said, "M-o-..."

Miss Bruce shook her head and said, "Please stop."

Real fast, Meaghan said, "Oh, oh—I know. I forgot to say the word first, right? Mouse; m-o..."

Shaking her head, Miss Bruce said, "I'm sorry, Meaghan, but you didn't follow the rules, and it's important that we all learn to follow directions exactly. So that means you are *out*."

Meaghan said, "But sometimes we get to

have a second chance. Because I know how to spell the word."

Miss Bruce didn't smile. She didn't even blink. She shook her head and said, "I believe it's very important to be thinking all the time. That's what I expect of myself, and I expect it of every one of you, too. I'm sorry, but you are *out*."

Miss Bruce looked down at the seating chart, but I kept looking at Meaghan. I felt bad for her. She was chewing on her bottom lip. She looked like she might even cry.

Miss Bruce looked up from the chart. She looked right at Willie and said, "Philip, the word is 'mouse.' "

Willie smiled and said, "Um, Miss Bruce? Everyone calls me Willie, 'cause my last name is Willis. And I like Willie better than Philip too. So you can call me Willie."

Miss Bruce looked at Willie and said, "When we get to know each other a little better, then perhaps I'll use your nickname. But for now, I'd like to use your real name, all right? Now, Philip, the first word is '*mouse.*'"

For a second Willie looked like he thought Miss Bruce was kidding about calling him Philip. But she just stood there with her eyebrows up, waiting. Then he knew it was for real.

Willie was so surprised he didn't know what to do. So he gulped once or twice. And then he gulped some more.

Miss Bruce said, "I guess Philip is not ready to play, so for this round Philip is *out.*" She looked down at the seating chart again, and then she looked right at me. "Jake, the first word is '*mouse.*' "

Maybe it was the look on Meaghan's face. Maybe it was the way Willie set there gulping. Or maybe it was the way Miss Bruce kept saying "*out*." I don't know what it was, but something inside my head snapped.

I looked right at Miss Bruce and in a high, squeaky voice I said, "Mouse: m-i-c-k-e-y; mouse."

It took a second before everyone figured out what I had spelled. Then it sounded like every kid in the room took a deep breath. And held it.

Miss Bruce stared at me through her big glasses. "That was *not* the right word!"

So I kept using my best Mickey Mouse voice, and I said, "Heh, heh—well then, I guess I'm *out*."

I also guessed I was in trouble. But part of

me didn't care.

Miss Bruce's face turned bright red. The paper in her hands started to shake. She looked like a cat when it's about to pounce.

Then Miss Bruce took three steps toward my chair. She frowned and said, "Jake, that was *not* funny!"

I took a quick look around the room. Everyone was grinning. And Willie was about to explode.

Miss Bruce was wrong. It *was* funny. Very funny.

Did Miss Bruce start yelling at me? Did she tell me to march down to the principal's office? Did she say, "I'll see *you* after school, Jake Drake!"

No.

Miss Bruce looked down at the seating chart. She kept looking at it for about five seconds—the longest five seconds of my life. And all that time I kept watching her face.

Then Miss Bruce looked up and said, "Annie, the word is still '*mouse.*' Spell it, please—*correctly.*"

And after Annie spelled it, Miss Bruce just went on with the spelling bee. *She acted like nothing had happened!*

But something had happened—actually, two things had happened:

The first thing was, I had done something silly in front of the whole class. Everybody had almost laughed out loud—they thought I was really funny! That had never happened before, and I kind of liked it. Plus, I hadn't gotten in trouble. Amazing!

The second thing that happened was more like a mystery. Because I wasn't really sure it had happened. It had happened—that is, *maybe* it had happened—when Miss Bruce was looking down at her seating chart, when I was watching her face. And here's the mystery: I thought I saw something.

Something I'd never seen before.

There on Miss Bruce's face. Just for a second.

And it had looked sort of like ... a *smile*.

CHAPTER FOUR

Secret Information

By the time we had library period on Monday, I was sure I'd made a mistake about what I saw on Friday. Miss Bruce smiling? Even a tiny little smile? No way.

All Monday morning we worked so hard. Miss Bruce pushed and pushed at us, every second. Math sheets, map skills, reading books, spelling drills. Even morning recess wasn't fun because we knew there was more work waiting for us. More work and no smiles.

But right before lunch we went to the library. Library period was great. A whole hour and tons of books. And no Miss Bruce. I mean, she was there, but she had to leave us alone for a while.

When we got there, I waved at Mrs. Brattle because she was helping in the library. She smiled and waved back.

Then I went to look for my Robin Hood Book.

Robin Hood was my favorite book back when I was in second grade. I had never checked it out, because then I probably would have finished reading it in two days. I only read it during library period. That way, it lasted longer. Like a good jawbreaker.

I knew right where to look, and the book was there.

All the soft chairs were filled up. Plus it was sort of noisy at the front of the media center. So I took my book to the back of the big room, where it was quiet.

I sat on the carpet between some shelves. I leaned against the wall. Then I opened the book, and there I was: Me and Robin Hood and Little John, riding our horses through Sherwood Forest.

I was really into the story when I heard someone say, "I have to talk with you." And the voice wasn't in my book. It was in the library.

And I knew that voice. It was Miss Bruce.

And I thought, *Great. I'm at the best part of my book, and she has to talk with me.*

I started to stand up. Then another voice

said, "All right, Hannah. We can talk right here."

And I knew that voice too. It was Mrs. Brattle. On the other side of the bookshelves. Three feet away.

I guess I could have made a noise. Or I could have stood up and started to look at the books on the shelf so they would see me.

But I didn't. I thought maybe I'd get in trouble for being way in the back of the library. Maybe they'd both yell at me.

So I froze. I just sat there.

I tried not to listen. I even put my hands over my ears. But I heard them anyway.

Mrs. Brattle said, "Sorry I didn't have time to talk with you on Friday afternoon. How's everything going?"

Miss Bruce said, "Well, something happened

right before lunch on Friday...and I'm not sure what to do about it."

"Oh?" said Mrs. Brattle. "What happened?"

And what did Miss Bruce talk about? She talked about me. She told Mrs. Brattle all about my big joke during the spelling bee.

And sitting there, I couldn't believe my ears. You know how you can tell a lot from hearing someone's voice? Well, even without seeing her, I could tell Miss Bruce was smiling. Smiling!

She even giggled a little and said, "I wish you could have seen Jake's face. He was *so* funny! He's such a cutie. I almost cracked up!"

Mrs. Brattle said, "Well, It's a good thing you didn't. Once you start laughing along with the kids, things can get out of hand very quickly."

"That's what my college teacher said too,"

said Miss Bruce. "She told us that the rule is, 'Don't smile until Christmas.' "

Mrs. Brattle chuckled and said, "Yes, I learned that too, and it's a good rule, especially when you're just starting out. Or when you're a substitute. Sometimes all it takes is one smile, and the kids will think they can get away with anything."

It was quiet for a few seconds. Then Miss Bruce said, "What do you think? Should I do something about Jake?"

"Jake?" said Mrs. Brattle. "Don't worry. He's a good boy. Still, you'll have to keep your eye on him. But if that's your biggest problem, then it sounds like you're doing just fine. Now, we'd better get back up front to the kids. It's getting a little too loud up there."

Then their voice got softer as they walked

away.

I sat there on the floor. My heart was pounding. My mouth was dry.

I crawled forward and peeked around the corner of the shelf. When no one was looking, I slipped out and moved to a different part of the library.

I felt like a second-grade spy. And now I had some secret information: Miss Bruce wasn't an alien. She knew how to smile. And giggle.

Plus, she thought I was a cutie.

And best of all, she thought I was *funny*.

When you're only eight years old, and you get this kind of secret information, it can start something.

And that something is called trouble.

CHAPTER FIVE

Unstoppable

All during lunch on Monday, I wanted to tell Willie. I wanted to tell him that Miss Bruce was a giggler. And that I was a cutie.

But I didn't. Because the best part of a secret is the part that makes it a secret. And that's keeping it.

Back in our room after lunch recess, I wasn't sure what to do. So for a while I didn't do anything. Except more work. Because right after lunch we had silent reading.

Miss Bruce told us to read a story in our reading books. Anyone who finished was supposed to read a second story. And anyone who finished the second story was supposed to read a third story. That way, the fast readers would keep busy while the slow readers were finishing the first story.

And then when everyone was done reading the first story, we were going to talk about it.

I was a pretty fast reader back in second grade, so I was almost done with the third story when Miss Bruce clapped her hands twice and said, "All right, class. Everyone please turn to page 77 in your reading book. Let's begin by talking about *who* was in this story." Miss Bruce looked down at the seating chart and said, "Andrea, can you tell us the name of one person who was in the story?"

And Andrea did. She said, "Jim."

Which wasn't so hard. There were only three people in the whole story. And the story was only twelve pages long. Plus it had lots of pictures.

Then Carlos told the next *who*, and Lisa told the last *who*.

So we were done with the *who* part. Which had been pretty boring. I thought Mrs. Brattle would have done it better.

But that's why Miss Bruce was there. So she could learn to be less boring. Someday. Maybe.

After the *who* came the *where*.

Miss Bruce said, "Now, tell the class *where* the story happened, Link."

Which was also super easy.

Except Link wasn't listening.

Link shoved something under the table and looked at Miss Bruce. And Link had that look in his eyes: the lost look.

Link said, "Um...where? Oh, yeah...where. Um...what was the question?"

Miss Bruce tilted her head and looked down at where Link had his hands under the table. Then her eyes got narrow and she pushed her lips together.

And I knew what was going to happen next. I could see it all: Miss Bruce was going to walk over and hold out her hand. Then she would say, "Link, give me that." And Link would pull out a comic book, or a toy, or something else really stupid. Then Miss Bruce would stare at him until he was really scared. She would make

Link feel bad about not paying attention. Just like she had done to Laura and Meaghan.

Back in second grade, Link wasn't very nice. Most of the time he was a bully. So it wasn't very often that I felt sorry for Link.

But I did. At that moment, I felt sorry for him. And I felt sort of mad at Miss Bruce. Because I felt like she was sort of being a bully too.

So before Miss Bruce had a chance to walk over to Link, I raised my hand and started waving it around.

Miss Bruce turned and looked at me.

She didn't want to call on me. I could tell she wasn't done with Link. I kept waving my hand in the air anyway.

So Miss Bruce said, "Yes, Jake?" She knew my name without looking at the seating chart.

I said, "I think I know where the story happened."

Miss Bruce wasn't sure what to do. She wanted to go after Link, but now she had called on me, and I had an answer. So she said, "Well, then...then tell us, Jake. Where?"

"Well...," I said slowly, "I'm not *exactly* sure..."

She said quickly, "Then just tell us where you *think* the story happened, Jake." Miss Bruce wanted to finish with me and get back to Link.

I said, "So I should just tell you? Like right now?"

She nodded her head at me.

Even slower, I said, "Even if I'm not *completely* sure?"

Miss Bruce said, "Yes, Jake. Even if it's only a guess. *Where* do you think this story happened?"

I looked Miss Bruce right in the eye and I said, "Well, I... I *think* it happened... on Earth!"

I kept staring into Miss Bruce's eyes. I heard a girl behind me giggle. But I didn't smile. I tried not to blink. I just waited.

Every kid in the room knew I had made a joke. Miss Bruce knew it too. But I kept acting like I was serious.

If she still thought I was a cutie, Miss Bruce did a good job of not showing it. She pushed her lips together into a thin line and glared at me. Then she said, "Yes. That's true. Of *course* the story happened on Earth, Jake." No smile. Not even a hint.

She turned back to Link. And now Link had his hand up. Whatever he had been hiding under the desk was gone.

Miss Bruce nodded at him and Link said, "The story happened by the ocean, right?"

"Yes, Link," said Miss Bruce. Then she took a deep breath. I thought she was going to walk over to Link and get mad at him anyway. Or maybe she would turn and get mad at me.

But she didn't. She let out her deep breath. Then she looked down at her seating chart again. She said, "Now, Ted, can you tell me *what* happened in our story?"

Ted was having a hard time. The corners of his mouth were wiggling. He wanted to smile, but he knew he'd better not.

I looked around the room. Half the kids in the class were smiling, and the other half were trying not to , like Ted.

There was only one person in the whole room who wasn't having any fun. And that was

Miss Bruce.

But I wasn't thinking about Miss Bruce, not right then. I was too busy. I was enjoying myself. Because for the second time in two days, I'd done something funny. And I'd gotten away with it both times!

I was the new class clown. I was unstoppable.

CHAPTER SIX

Mr. Funny Bone

When I got home from school on Monday afternoon, I asked my mom if I could have a snack. Because being so funny had made me hungry.

So Mom made me some peanut butter on crackers. Plus a glass of milk.

As I was eating I started to think. I tried to remember other times I had been funny at school. Like back when I was in first grade. Or kindergarten. I tried to remember. And I couldn't think of any.

And now, all of sudden, I had made everyone want to start laughing—twice! And it had been so easy. I hadn't even been trying that hard.

I stopped right in the middle of drinking my milk. And I thought to myself, *If you're this funny without even trying, think how funny you could be if you worked at it!* I decided I could probably become the funniest kid in the history of the universe! And I could start the very next day!

If I was going to be super funny, I'd need super jokes. And I'd have to tell them just right.

So I went to find Abby. She's my little sister. When I was in second grade, Abby was in kindergarten. I found her in her room listening to a story cassette of *The Three Little Pigs.*

I went over to the cassette player and shut it off.

Abby said, "Hey! Put it back on!"

"Wait," I said, "because I want to try telling you some jokes. Okay?"

Abby crossed her arms and frowned. "I don't want jokes. I want the pigs."

"C'mon," I said. "It'll be fun. Are you ready?"

Abby scratched her knee. And made a face at the ceiling. And sat up on the edge of her bed. Then she said, "Okay."

So I said, "Knock, knock."

Abby wrinkled her nose. She said, "What?"

"I said, 'Knock, knock.' You know—it's a knock-knock joke."

Abby shook her head. "That's not funny."

"That's 'cause the joke's not over yet. Listen," I said, "I say 'Knock, knock,' then you say

'Who's there?', okay?" Then I said, "Knock, knock."

And Abby said, "Who's there, okay?"

"No," I said. "You just say 'Who's there?' That's all you say. Just 'Who's there?' Now let's try it again. Ready?"

Abby nodded her head.

So I said, "Knock, knock."

And Abby said, "Who's there?"

And I said, "Toodle."

And Abby laughed. She clapped her hands and said, "Toodle's funny. Tell another one."

"No, no," I said. "Toodle' isn't the funny part. I say 'Knock, knock.' Then you say 'Who's there?' Then I say 'Toodle,' and then you say 'Toodle *who?*' and *then* I finish the joke."

Abby looked at me. She said, "Toodle *was* funny. I don't want more joke."

"C' mon," I said. "I have to finish it, okay? I'm going to start over again."

Abby frowned. "Don't want to."

But I said, "Knock, knock."

And Abby said, "Who's there, okay?"

"No!" I yelled. "You just say 'Who's there?' Get it right, Abby!"

Abby shook her head. And then she yelled, "Mommeeee! MOMMEEEEE!" Abby can really yell.

Mom ran up the stairs and into Abby's room in about two seconds. "What's the matter—are you hurt?" Then Mom saw me. She said, "Oh! Jake. Good. You're here too. Is everyone all right? Why did you call me like that, Abby?"

Abby pointed at me. "Because of him. He won't tsop making a joke."

Mom frowned at me. "Have you been teasing

Abby again, Jake?"

"No!" I said. "I'm not teasing her. I'm just trying to tell one stupid little knock-knock joke. And she can't even do it. And it's driving me crazy!"

Mom said, "Well, why don't you tell me the knock-knock joke. Then Abby can listen and see how it works, all right?"

I said, "Okay. Knock, knock."

And Mom said, "Who's there?"

And I said, "Toodle."

And Mom said, "Toodle who?"

And I said, "Toodle-oo to you too!"

Mom smiled and nodded. She said, "That's a good one."

Abby shook her head. "No. just toodle. Toodle was better."

And that's when I went to my room. To

practice telling jokes by myself.

I stood in front of the mirror that's above my dresser. I looked at myself and I started telling jokes.

Knock, knock.

Who's there?

Seven, eight, nine.

Seven, eight, nine who?

Sven ate nine cookies!

Knock, knock.

Who's there?

Robins go.

Robins go who?

No! Robins go tweet; *owls* **go who!**

What goes "Ha Ha bonk"?

 56

A man who laughs his head off!

If I had five baseballs in one hand,
and I had five baseballs in the other,
what would I have?
Really BIG hands!

What's worse than finding a worm in
your apple?
Finding half a worm!

It's not much fun telling jokes to yourself, so I got tired of that pretty fast. But as I looked in the mirror, I remembered how great I am at making funny faces.

So I practiced crossing my eyes and sticking my tongue out. I practiced pushing my nose up and making a pig face. I practiced puffing up my cheeks and pulling my eyelids out of shape. No doubt about it: I was a pretty funny kid.

But after a while my face got tired. And my eyes started to hurt from crossing them so much.

So I looked on my bookshelf until I found this book of jokes I got at a book fair. And I sat on my bed and I read the whole book. Then I lay down on my stomach and read it again. The whole book.

I guess being so funny had made me tired, because I fell asleep with my face in the joke book. And the next thing I knew, Mom was calling to me to come downstairs for dinner.

When I went into the kitchen, my dad smiled at me and said, "Hey, Jake! What's new?"

And I said, "The moon."

Dad said, "The moon?"

And I said, "Yup. There's a new moon every month."

Dad and Mom laughed, and Dad said, "That's a good one, Jake."

Abby said, "It's not as funny as toodle."

We all sat at the table and I looked at the food. Right away I said, "Hey, Mom, know what they make from lazy cows? Meatloaf! Get it? Loaf? Like lazy? I just made that up! Pretty funny, huh?"

Mom smiled and nodded as she passed the potatoes. "Yes, pretty funny, Jake."

Then I said, "Hey, Dad, know how come the farmer ran a steamroller across his fields?"

Dad smiled and shook his head. So I said, "Because he wanted to grow some mashed potatoes!"

Dad laughed and said, "Mashed potatoes!

That's a good one!"

All during dinner the jokes just kept on coming. It was like anything I looked at turned into a joke. Sometimes I remembered jokes, and sometimes I made up new ones. I even made my fish face at Abby when she was drinking her milk. Which made a big mess. But that was funny too!

When we had dessert, I said, "Hey, Dad, do you use your right hand or your left hand when you eat ice cream?"

"I guess I use my right hand."

And I said, "That's funny—I always use a *spoon!*"

I was hilarious!

When I asked to be excused, Dad said, "You sure are Mr. Funny Bone tonight, Jake. How'd all this get started?"

And like a dope I said, "Oh, it started at school."

Wrong thing to say.

Right away Dad frowned. He said, "Well, I hope you're getting it all out of your system before tomorrow morning. Being funny like this at school isn't a good idea, Jake. You understand that, right?"

And I nodded and I said, "Oh, I know that." And that was true. Because I knew it wasn't a good idea.

No, being funny at school on Tuesday wasn't a *good* idea: It was a *great* idea!

CHAPTER SEVEN

Christmas in April

On Tuesday morning Miss Bruce piled on the work. All my practice being Mr. Funny Bone wasn't any help at all. We had so much to do that I didn't have a chance to tell a single joke.

Plus, Miss Bruce was acting grumpier and grumpier.

When we were doing some math work, Carlos got up and started walking to the back of the room.

Miss Bruce looked at him and said, "Carlos, please stay in your seat and keep working. Math time is almost over."

He held up his pencil. "Gotta sharpen this."

Miss Bruce said, "I'm sure it's fine for now. Please keep working."

Carlos said, "But my pencil has to be extra sharp when I do math. It helps me make good numbers."

Miss Bruce said, "What did I tell you to do, Carlos?"

Carlos said, "You told me to sit down. But I need my pencil sharper. Honest."

Miss Bruce said, "You're wasting time, Carlos, and you have to finish all your math problems. So sit. Get back to work. Now."

Carlos walked slowly back to his chair and

sat down.

Right away Annie reached across the table and handed Carlos a pencil.

Miss Bruce looked at Annie and she said, "Annie! *What* are you doing?"

Annie froze. She couldn't speak.

Miss Bruce said, "Annie, answer me!"

So Annie sort of hunched her shoulders and said, "I had an extra pencil. A sharp one."

Miss Bruce frowned, and I thought she was going to start yelling. But she said, "Fine. That was very nice of you, Annie. Now, get back to work, both of you. Because anyone who does not finish all the math problems will have to stay in during recess."

Miss Bruce was acting so grumpy that I kind of got scared again. It was like my dad had said: Trying to be funny at school didn't seem like a good idea. I wanted to tell some jokes, but I didn't want to run in front of a train. And at that moment Miss Bruce seemed a lot like a locomotive.

So I finished my math problems, and so did everyone else. Then Miss Bruce told us to take out our spelling workbooks. And we did. And then Miss Bruce told us to turn to page 62. And we did. And we got right to work.

The spelling work was easy. It's the kind of work that leaves plenty of room inside your head for other stuff. So I started thinking about how funny I had been at dinner the night before.

And sitting there copying over words that end with "tch," I remembered something I'd forgotten to practice at home. Something very funny. Something I'm great at: noises.

Like my mouth-pops. I can make this really

loud POP by pulling my tongue off the roof of my mouth. It's a great noise.

And I also make a good duck sound. I can quack by pushing air out of one side of my mouth. Plus I can laugh sort of like Donald Duck.

But my best sound is the one I always practice when Willie and I have sleepovers. And that's burping. Willie's a pretty good burper too, but I'm a better burper.

To make a big burp, all you have to do is gulp some air down into your stomach. And then you let it come back out as a burp. Simple.

So I was sitting there on that Tuesday morning doing my spelling work. Plus thinking about burping.

I wrote *patch*. And then I took a gulp of air.

I wrote *catch*. And I took a gulp of air.

I wrote *latch*. And I took a gulp of air.

I wrote *pitch*. Another gulp of air.

I wrote *ditch*. And I took one more gulp of air.

It wasn't until I took that fifth gulp of air that I remembered something. I wasn't at a sleepover at Willie's house. I was at school.

I straightened up in my chair and leaned back a little. It felt like I had a balloon. stuffed under my T-shirt. But it wasn't a balloon. It was my stomach. I tapped on it with my pencil. It made a hollow sound, sort of like a tom-tom.

And that's when Miss Bruce came right up behind me and said, "Are you all done with your work, Jake?"

I turned around real fast and looked up into her face. And I said, "Nope."

That's what I *tried* to say. But I *actually* said,

"NOOOOOOOOOOOOOOOOOOOOOOOOOOOOPE."

It was the longest, loudest burp of my life!

The classroom was completely quiet. Everyone stared at me. Including Miss Bruce.

Don't ask me how I got the idea to do what I did next, because I don't know. There was Miss Bruce with her arms folded, looking down at me through her huge black glasses, and what did I do? I patted my chest, and I crossed my eyes, and I said, "Pardon me! It must have been that frog I ate for breakfast!"

Miss Bruce stood there. She was trying to get mad. She wanted to frown and yell and shake her finger at me and tell me that I had been terribly, terribly rude.

But she couldn't. I was just too funny. Plus I was a cutie.

So what did Miss Bruce do? She smiled!

And it wasn't a little smile. It was a great big smile with teeth and everything. It was almost a grin. Every kid in the class saw that smile. And they also heard her giggle.

Miss Bruce's teacher at college had said, "Don't smile until Christmas." On that April morning, I was Santa Claus. Christmas had arrived!

After Miss Bruce smiled and giggled, everybody laughed a little. Then Miss Bruce covered her mouth with her hand and shook her head. And she tried to look serious again.

She said, "Let's not get silly, class. Please keep working on your spelling ." And it almost worked. We all started to quiet down.

Then Willie burped almost as loud as I had and said, "I had *two* frogs for breakfast!"

All the kids laughed at that, much louder,

and Susan Tuttle said, "Oooh! Gross!"

When a class starts laughing, it's sort of like when a volcano begins to rumble. Because it doesn't seem like much at first, but it's still dangerous.

Miss Bruce clapped her hands twice and said, "Class, that's enough!"

But the class didn't think it was enough. We were just getting started.

Link Baxter stood up and put his hands up under his arms and started hopping around the back of the room. "Hey, look! Look! I'm a frog. Ribbet! Ribbet!"

Miss Bruce clapped again. "Link, sit down! All of you, be quiet!"

No one was listening. Willie was still burping. Link was still hopping around the back of the room.

Then Ted tossed a ball of paper at Ben, and Ben threw it back to him. Carlos waved his arms and called, "Hey, Ted! Ted! Over here!"

And they started to play keep-away while Annie and Meaghan called out "Yay, Ben! Yay, Carlos! Hey, toss it to us, too!"

Miss Bruce shouted, "QUIET!"

But it kept getting louder and louder and louder. Our room had turned into an erupting volcano of laughing and shouting and goofing around.

And once that kind of volcano gets going, there's usually only one thing that can stop it: a real teacher.

Except there is one other way to plug the volcano. I saw it happen that morning.

Because if a student teacher stamps her feet and screams, "Stop it! Stop it!" and then bursts out crying and runs out of the classroom and slams the door, the volcano shuts down. And the room gets quiet.

Very, very quiet.

CHAPTER EIGHT

Judge Brattle

Mrs. Brattle walked into the room two minutes after Miss Bruce had run out.

Twenty-three kids were doing spelling work.

Silently.

No one even looked up at Mrs. Brattle. No one dared.

Mrs. Brattle sat down at the front of the

room. She tapped a pencil on her desk and said, "Please stop working."

When we were all looking at her, she said, "Now, who will tell me what happened in here? With Miss Bruce."

Mrs. Brattle was wearing a white shirt and a black sweater. She looked like a lady judge on one of those TV shows. Judge Brattle. She tapped her pencil on her desk again and looked around the room. She said, "I'm waiting..."

I wanted to stand up and say, "Your Honor, it was all my fault. I'm just too funny. And I knew that Miss Bruce was a secret giggler. And I didn't mean to burp, but after I did, I said that thing about the frog. And that's what got everything so crazy. And I'm sorry that I'm so hilarious."

But I didn't say that. I didn't say anything.

Instead, Marsha McCall raised her hand. And when Mrs. Brattle called on her, Marsha started talking. And she talked in questions like she always does. She said, "Well, we were working on our spelling lessons? Because you know how it's Tuesday? And you know Miss Bruce? How she started laughing after Jake burped? Well, you know how it's hard to stop laughing sometimes? Don't you think maybe that's what happened? That everybody couldn't stop laughing?"

Marsha said a lot of words, but Mrs. Brattle only heard three of them. Mrs. Brattle turned and looked at me. And she said, " 'After Jake burped?' Did Marsha just say 'after Jake burped'? Tell me a little more about that part of the story, Jake."

So I said, "I didn't mean to. But I did. Burp.

And it was a big burp too. And then I said something funny."

Mrs. Brattle raised her eyebrows. She said, "Something funny?"

I nodded. "Yeah. I guess it was funny. I said it must have been the frog I ate for breakfast."

The corners of Mrs. Brattle's mouth wiggled a little, but she didn't smile. She said, "I see. And then what happened?"

"It just started to get silly. In the room. After Miss Bruce smiled. Because she never smiled at all until then. Not even once. And then she laughed a little too. And then...it got loud. That's all."

I guess I could have told Mrs. Brattle how Ted and Ben had been throwing stuff and how the girls had been yelling and how Willie had kept burping and Link kept hopping around.

But I didn't. Because I knew none of that would have happened if I hadn't been so funny. It was all my fault.

I guess that's what Mrs. Brattle thought too. Because she stood up and said, "Class, Mrs. Reed is on her way here. While she's here, I want you to finish your spelling and then you may do some silent reading. *Silent* reading."

Then she turned and looked at me. She said, "Jake, stand up. You're coming with me."

As we walked out of the courtroom, Judge Brattle didn't smile.

And neither did I.

CHAPTER NINE

No More Clowning

I thought Judge Brattle was taking me to jail.
Which would have been the principal's office.

So I was surprised when she marched right
past the office. Instead, she stopped at a door
marked TEACHERS' ROOM. She opened the
door and said, "In here, Jake."

I'd never been in the teachers' room before.
It was pretty nice in there. There was a big

couch and a refrigerator. There was a little table in front of the couch with sone megazines on it. One wall was covered with a huge bulletin board. Which was kind of messy. There was a big bookcase. There was even a Coke machine. Definitely the best room in the whole school.

And sitting at the big table in the middle of the room was Miss Bruce. With a box of tissues. And a red nose.

Miss Bruce's big glasses were next to the box of tissues. Without her glasses on, Miss Bruce looked like she was in high school. Just a girl with puffy eyes and a runny nose.

Mrs. Brattle pulled out a chair for me across from Miss Bruce. She walked around the table and sat down next to her student teacher.

Then Mrs. Brattle said, "Jake, is there something you want to say to Miss Bruce?"

I wanted to say, "Knock, knock." Because Miss Bruce looked like she needed a joke to cheer her up. But I knew that wasn't a good idea. So I said what Mrs. Brattle wanted me to. I said, "I'm sorry I was so funny in class. And I'm sorry I made you giggle. By being so funny."

Miss Bruce dabbed at her eyes and said, "It's okay, Jake. I'm sorry I got so upset. I didn't want to. And I shouldn't have. But it's all over now. So it's okay."

Mrs. Brattle shook her hand and said, "Actually, it's not okay, Miss Bruce. Jake shouldn't have been trying to do anything except be good and get his work done. Right, Jake?" I nodded. "And if you make a rude noise by mistake, then all you need to say is 'Excuse me.' Is that clear?" I nodded again. Mrs. Brattle narrowed her eyes and looked right into my face. "Jake, it *was* a mistake, right? When you burped?"

And I looked right back into Mrs. Brattle's eyes. And I was so glad that I could tell the truth, because Judge Brattle would have been able to tell I was lying. I said, "Yes. I didn't burp on purpose."

Mrs. Brattle nodded. "I'm glad to know that, at least. But the silliness has got to stop. Now. Do you understand?"

I nodded. "Uh-huh. No more silliness."

Mrs. Brattle said, "All right, then. Miss Bruce, is there anything else you want to say?"

Miss Bruce shook her head. She looked a lot better. But I could still tell she had been crying. She said, "No. Nothing else."

Then Mrs. Brattle said, "Jake, how about

you? Anything else?"

It was one of those times when I should have known to keep my mouth shut. I should have just shaken my head and sat there looking scared. Or maybe I should have whispered "No , thank you," and folded my hands in my lap. But I didn't.

I looked right at Miss Bruce and I said, "Miss Bruce, how come you never smiled until today? Was that because of what your teacher said? About Christmas?"

Oops. BIG oops! The second I said that I knew I had mad a major goof.

Miss Bruce's eyes opened wide. And so did Mrs. Brattle's. They both looked at me. And then they looked at each other. And then back at me. Mrs. Brattle folded her arms.

And I knew they knew. They knew I had

heard them talking that day in the library.

Miss Bruce sat up straight in her chair. Even without the big glasses, her eyes were plenty scary. She said, "Why...why you little *sneak!* You were *spying* on me!" I was glad she was over on the other side of the big table.

I gulped and said real fast, "No, really, I wasn't spying! That day in the library? I didn't mean to hear you talking. I didn't do it on purpose. I was just sitting there reading *Robin Hood*, and you came to where I was, and I was afraid I'd get in trouble for sitting in the back, and then you started talking. You just started talking! I tried not to listen. But I heard you anyway. I didn't mean to. And I didn't tell anyone about it. Honest! And I'm sorry." I was looking back and forth between their faces.

I could tell they believed me. But I still felt

like Miss Bruce was going to jump over the table and come after me.

Mrs. Brattle took charge. She said, "Seems like you have quite a lot to be sorry about today, Jake. But I think Miss Bruce and I understand the situation. And, if Miss Bruce will accept your apology, then so will I, and we'll just put all of this business behind us. All right, Miss Bruce?"

Miss Bruce nodded. But it wasn't a very big nod.

"Very well, then," said Mrs. Brattle, standing up. "Then let's get you two back to class."

Miss Bruce kind of jumped a little in her chair. "Me?" she asked. "You mean I have to go back? To your class? Today?"

Mrs. Brattle looked down at Miss Bruce and smiled. "Why, of course you do. Right now.

You're the teacher."

Mrs. Bruce looked like someone had just told her to go for a walk in a graveyard. At midnight. Without a flashlight. She was scared.

And then I got it: She was scared of *us*—of the kids! Of noise and silliness and craziness! Miss Bruce was scared, and Mrs. Brattle wasn't. Because Mrs. Brattle was a real teacher.

Miss Bruce bit her lip. She looked at Mrs. Brattle and said, "Don't you think you should come with me?"

Mrs. Brattle shook her head. "No, you'll be fine. The class will be waiting to see what happened to Jake, and Jake is going to look like he's had a good scolding. Jake is also going to be a perfect *angel* from this moment on. And *you* are going to walk back into that room and show all the boys and girls that just because you smile once in a while does not mean that they can go wild and misbehave."

Miss Bruce said, "But...but I *cried*. All those kids saw me cry and run out of the room! I *can't* go back."

Mrs. Brattle smiled and patted Miss Bruce on the arm. "Don't worry, dear. Everyone understands about crying, especially children. When it happens, you dry your face off, and then you go on with whatever you have to do. And *you* have a class to teach."

Then Mrs. Brattle took hold of the back of Miss Bruce's chair, so Miss Bruce had to stand up.

"There we go," said Mrs. Brattle. "Now, you and Jake run along. Mrs. Reed is needed back in the library. And Jake, from now on, I want nothing but good news about you, is that clear?"

I nodded.

And then Miss Bruce and I walked down the hall to our classroom.

I did what Mrs. Brattle said. I walked into the room. I sat down. I didn't look at anybody. I didn't smile. I tried to look like I had just lived through the worst ten minutes of my life. I tried to look like I was happy just to be alive.

And it turned out that Mrs. Brattle was right. Not one kid tried to be silly. Not one kid was noisy or rude.

And Miss Bruce did great. After all that yelling and the crying and the running out of the room, she acted like it wasn't a big deal. And because she acted that way, it wasn't. It was like none of it had ever happened.

But it had happened. And I had the proof. Because I kept on being funny.

Except I was never funny in class. And not when Miss Bruce was around. Or Mrs. Brattle.

So mostly I was funny for Willie. Before school, at recess, in gym class, on Saturdays— every chance I got, I told Willie jokes and made funny noises and faces at him. At lunch one day I made a pig face, and Willie laughed so hard he snorted a chunk of Oreo right out of his nose! I was a riot!

But after about three weeks, Willie was starting to go crazy, and I was starting to run out of jokes. So one day I just stopped. And I'm glad I did, because it's hard to try to be funny *all* the time. It's much better to save up silliness for special occasions. Like sleepovers. Or long bus rides.

The rest of Miss Bruce's student-teaching time went by pretty fast. And then the best part is she wasn't as grumpy or as picky or as fussy as before. It was like Miss Bruce didn't have to be that way anymore. Because she wasn't afraid. I guess if you can laugh and giggle, and then watch your class go nuts, and then scream and yell, and then run out of the room crying, and *then* come back and have everything be okay, there's not much left to be scared about.

Mrs. Brattle planned a surprise party for Miss Bruce at the end of her three weeks. We all signed a big card we made for her in art class. And when Mrs. Brattle gave her a book and a hug, I thought Miss Bruce was going to start crying and run out of the room again.

But she didn't. she blinked a lot. And then she smiled. It was a big smile, with teeth and everything. Her voice sounded wobbly. And she said, "I learned so much here at Despres Elementary School. And I know that no matter how many other places I go and no matter how many other children I teach, I'm never going to forget you."

Miss Bruce was talking to the whole class. But at the end, she looked right at me. And I got this feeling that what she meant was, she was never going to forget me: Jake Drake, Class Clown.

我是傑克，
天才搞笑王

我是傑克，
天才搞笑王

文◎安德魯・克萊門斯
譯◎黃筱茵　圖◎唐唐

國家圖書館出版品預行編目（CIP）資料

我是傑克，天才搞笑王 / 安德魯.克萊門斯（Andrew
　Clements）文; 黃筱茵譯; 唐唐圖. --初版. --臺北市:
　遠流, 2014.05
　　面;　公分. --（安德魯.克萊門斯; 16）
　　譯自 : Jake Drake, class clown
　　ISBN 978-957-32-7409-4（平裝附光碟片））

874.59　　　　　　　　　　　　103006605

安德魯‧克萊門斯16
我是傑克，天才搞笑王

文 / 安德魯‧克萊門斯　譯 / 黃筱茵　圖 / 唐唐

主編 / 林孜懃　編輯協力 / 盧珮如、丘瑾　內頁設計 / 邱銳致
行銷企劃 / 陳佳美　出版一部總編輯暨總監 / 王明雪

發行人 / 王榮文
出版發行 / 遠流出版事業股份有限公司　台北市南昌路2段81號6樓
電話：(02)2392-6899　傳真：(02)2392-6658　郵撥：0189456-1
著作權顧問 / 蕭雄淋律師　法律顧問 / 董安丹律師
輸出印刷 / 中原造像股份有限公司
□ 2014年 5 月 1 日　初版一刷
□ 2020年10月30日　初版六刷

行政院新聞局局版台業字第1295號
定價 / 新台幣260元 (缺頁或破損的書，請寄回更換)
有著作權‧侵害必究　Printed in Taiwan
ISBN　978-957-32-7409-4
遠流博識網 http://www.ylib.com　E-mail:ylib@ylib.com
遠流YA讀報粉絲團 https://www.facebook.com/yaread

【推薦導讀一】
進入兒童的大人世界

實踐大學應外系講座教授

陳超明

在《傑克與魔豆》的童話故事中，聰明伶俐的傑克（Jack），運用智慧，巧奪巨人的財富；而在現今的校園裡，不同的傑克（Jake），也面臨不一樣的巨人，正要開始現實生活的冒險之旅。

當自己故事的主人翁

每個人小時候，大都擁有聽大人說故事或自己讀故事的喜悅！

沉浸在故事的幻想世界裡，不管是小飛俠彼得潘在森林飛舞，還是孫悟空作弄不同妖魔鬼怪，或傑克與巨人間的最後對抗，我們小小的心靈，都暫時脫離父母的嘮叨、學校作業的負擔、隔壁小胖的霸凌，愉快的當自己的主人翁。

從另一面看事情，問題就解決了

　　故事永遠是我們心靈的好夥伴；好的故事，更是我們展現想像力的好場所！將故事結合現實面，這套【我是傑克】系列，帶我們進入「兒童的大人世界」。我們跟隨著主人翁傑克，有如巨人世界的傑克般，進入各種學校與生活冒險。聰明善良的傑克不斷摸索，發掘事情的另一面，找到破解的方法。

　　大家常常說，小孩是個無憂無慮的天使。真的是如此嗎？這些故事顛覆了我們大人的看法。回想一下，我們小時候在學校裡，是不是也要面對很多成長的挑戰：不同階段的霸凌、太聰明或太愚蠢的煩惱、同學老師的排擠或另眼相看？故事裡，傑克願意面對自己的問題，也認識自己有限的能力。故事中常不經意的批評大人的輕忽與便宜行事，往往成為小孩世界的夢魘。

迷人的說故事能力

作者是個說故事高手，以第一人稱的敘述觀點進入小孩的世界，勾劃出這些學校的夢魘，更製造層層高潮，吸引我們閱讀：傑克如何打敗超級霸凌者？傑克如何對抗「師寶」的封號？傑克如何鍛鍊自己的智力？傑克又如何發現老師的另一面？小孩的「成熟」，對照大人的「無知」，正是這些故事迷人的地方。誠如傑克自己所說，他一直搞不懂，學校這些每天在教導他們的大人不是應該很聰明、很厲害嗎？為什麼他們始終沒辦法解決校園霸凌的問題呢？不管是大人，還是小孩，來閱讀這些小孩或大人間的精采互動，都會覺得非常有趣！

如何閱讀本系列作品

【我是傑克】不僅是教導小孩如何找到解決問題的方法，更是

學習語言的好故事書。作者簡潔的語言與故事間的精采轉折，都是本書成功的地方。遠流出版，保留其英文原文，是個非常聰明的作法。我們可以閱讀中文，了解故事情節，也可以回頭看英文，品味這些簡潔語言帶來的美感與魅力。例如 "I tried to smile and nod at him, but I know I looked kind of spooked, because I was spooked. And Link could see I was spooked. And he liked it. And that's when I knew I was in big bully-trouble." 短短四句，重複 spooked，一方面交待傑克成為霸凌對象的過程，一方面也點出其內心的驚慌。這種精采句子到處可見，值得細讀。

這是一系列情節緊湊、語言簡潔、啟發性強的少年故事，大人、小孩都可一起閱讀，不但可以幫助你學習語言，也可以協助你好好面對問題、解決問題！

【推薦導讀二】

給讀【我是傑克】的你們

兒童文學作家

辛佳慧

親愛的，我猜，你拿到這本書，可能是父母長輩買來或找來給你的，也可能是同學推薦的。不管怎樣，我們因此在這裡、這一頁相遇。你正讀著字，讀著我這個推薦導讀人寫的字……我的工作就是好好的向你介紹這系列的四本書，就像你的一個好朋友發現了好東西時，會急著和你分享一樣。

安德魯・克萊門斯是美國一位擅長寫學校故事的作家，他總能以學生觀點捉摸到學校生活的各種面相，所以他寫的故事在美國很受歡迎。因為小讀者不會覺得作家藉機說道理（我完全可以體會你們聽說教故事的心情，那感覺就像一朵花好端端的被強行帶到沙漠裡一樣，令人煎熬難受），而是懂得你們的處境或心理，隨著你們

的眼睛去感受學校會發生的事情。那種感覺，就像作家透過文字的魔法讓你們變成一尾尾小魚，跳入小溪、滑入大海去自在悠游，卻同時能帶領你們看到特別的新景物。

【我是傑克】這系列講的是一個小男生在他小學不同年級所發生的故事，每本書就像一片片不同的海域，讓小魚兒帶著熟悉的安全感與新鮮的好奇心去探索。

《我是傑克，霸凌終結者》是在說鎮上新來的一個小惡霸，而且他偏偏挑中傑克當他欺負的對象。這讓傑克有機會回想自己為何老是成為惡霸磁鐵，並且激起他要當霸凌終結者的鬥志。不知道你有沒有被霸凌或霸凌別人的經驗？我幼稚園時，有好幾次被霸凌的經驗，那種恐怖心情，一直到現在還記著呢。你們呢？有思考過為何會發生霸凌，發生了要怎麼應對嗎？

《我是傑克，完美馬屁精》這本也是說著我們都熟悉的情境。

我自己就學期間，從幼稚園到博士班都不喜歡那種會巴結老師或討老師歡心的學生，也就是老師眼中的寵物，同學眼中的馬屁精。不過，有時候你偏偏就會被某個老師盯上，他會對你很好，開口閉口都是你，這讓你很困擾，因為你不想被老師馴服、被同學排擠，你想和同學們同一國，卻不知道該怎麼辦？喔，相信我，那可沒那麼簡單，絕對比把期末考考好還要難，但卻有意思極了！

另外，你有沒有過這種經驗？眼前有個大賽，比的正是你的長項，而且獎品非常非常吸引你，為了得獎，你於是進入了一種六親不認、全力以赴，卻又疑神疑鬼的狀態。整個過程很煎熬，考驗著你和家人、同學的關係，也衝擊著自己對自己的信心，但同時一路上也可能出現意外而有趣的路口，等著你轉彎過去！如果有，那你

一定要讀《我是傑克，超跩萬事通》這一本。

另一本《我是傑克，天才搞笑王》也描述了我小時候在學校經歷過的事，就是你明明知道在老師面前「乖乖的」便可以沒事，但你還是忍不住「搞怪」。你也知道下一刻因此要惹禍上身，卻意外觀察到老師們有異狀，然後你才慢慢發現，其實他們有另一個不是老師的身份存在。這個新發現讓你重新看待自己和大人的關係，也才知道原來上學這件事有好笑、溫柔與不為人知的一面呢！

總之，我很努力的向你們介紹這四本書有意思且吸引人的地方，希望你接下去有機會翻完它們，並回過頭來評評我分享的話有沒有道理。若覺得沒道理，那也很好，這樣你就可以開始寫你想分享給其他小讀者的推薦導讀了，我可是很樂意拜讀的！

名家好評推薦

乖巧、伶俐，帶著一點膽怯，卻又總是強自鎮定的傑克，和我兒子正好同年，今年十歲，四年級。而且，有點小聰明的性格也有那麼一點類似呢！所以，每當我看到傑克在學校裡遇到麻煩與困擾時，忍不住也會想像，當我兒子遇到同樣情形時，他會怎麼辦？

克萊門斯的作品活潑逗趣，貼近小朋友的想法與經歷，讀來輕鬆愉快，又引人入勝。【我是傑克】系列以中英語方式出版，拉長了閱讀年齡層，讓高年級的孩子也可以把它當成一本練習英文的讀本，是相當值得收藏的好書喔！

──親子作家

陳安儀

1 新老闆

我是傑克，全名叫傑克‧德瑞克。我只有十歲，可是我已經有全職工作了，因為我就是那樣看待上學這件事，那就是我的工作。

我現在四年級，所以我做同一個工作已經超過五年了。

如果你一件事做得夠久，就會變得很內行，這也是為什麼我會開始變成一個校園專家。

我是傑克，天才搞笑王

我到現在已經有過一堆不同的老闆，因為老師其實就是老闆。而且有一件事我很確定，如果你的老闆總是一臉不高興，那實在有夠悶。

到目前為止，事情都還過得去。我有幾個老師會不時發飆，其中幾個有時還真的會大吼大叫。今年我四年級的導師是湯普森先生，他有時候會脾氣暴躁，再加上他的耳朵還長了咖啡色的毛，所以他有可能是個狼人。

儘管如此，我還不曾碰過真正整天繃著臉的導師——至少不是一整學年都碰到啦。

不過威利可就沒這麼好運了。威利是我最好的朋友，去年他三年級的導師是佛魯太太，她是那種會鐵著一張臉四處

18

走動的老闆，就像一隻貓在外面淋著雨的模樣。如果你走過她的教室，會覺得自己好像應該小聲說話、踮腳尖走路，因為只要佛魯太太看你一眼，她就能找到讓她發飆的事。

所以三年級對威利來說很不好過，因為他是那種愛笑的小孩。把佛魯太太和威利擺在同一間教室是個糟糕的主意。

三年級的第一天，我在午餐時間遇到威利，就可以感覺到有些事情不對勁。他看起來有點蒼白，一副好像要暈過去之類的模樣。我說：「嘿，你還好嗎？」

他說：「不，我不好，佛魯太太已經討厭我了。她早上花了一半的時間對我大吼大叫，另一半的時間，我都在試著搞清楚到底哪裡做錯了。」

我問：「發生什麼事？」

威利聳聳肩。「我就是不知道啊。我什麼都沒做，只是坐在那裡，突然看見佛魯太太在看我，所以我對她笑一笑，然後她就皺著眉頭說：『年輕人，拿掉你臉上那種笑容。』所以我就照做，像這樣把手抹過嘴巴，沒有再笑。可是那個動作讓羅比・坎森開始笑，然後佛魯太太就氣炸了。她叫我站起來，走去穿堂。之後她走出來，彎下腰，幾乎貼上我的臉，近到我都可以直接往上看到她的鼻子。她對我搖搖手指，然後說：『如果你下次還敢在我的教室裡自作聰明，你就會非常、非常後悔！』」

可憐的傢伙，那只不過是威利三年級的第一天耶，後來

狀況也沒有變得比較好。整整一年，佛魯太太每星期最少會

對威利吼三次，而且他是那種**好**孩子耶！像是傑·卡恩斯和

札克·沃爾騰那些小孩呢？就是那些真的搗蛋鬼啊。對那些

傢伙來說，待在佛魯太太班上就和關在戰俘營裡沒兩樣。說

不定還更慘，因為在戰俘營裡，就算你搞砸了，也不必拿警

告單叫你的家長簽名。

　　我三年級的導師是斯納文太太，她大部分時間人很好。

真希望威利能換到我班上，可是事情不是那樣運作的，只要

學期一開始，你就得一整年和你的導師黏在一起，而你只能

盡力而為。

　　威利就是那樣做，他三年級時過得不太開心，可是他撐

過去了。就連傑和札克也活下來了，因為當你的老師是個暴躁鬼時，你只能這麼做。你學會了要活下去該怎麼做，而你就這樣做了。你知道只需要這個學年結束，就再也不會遇到同一個老闆，所以你只要盡力而為，並等到夏天。

就像我說的，我大部分的老師人都不錯。事實上，我目前為止遇過脾氣最暴躁的老師甚至不算是老師。她是實習老師，她教我的時間沒有很久，大概只有三個禮拜，那樣已經夠久了。她叫做布魯斯小姐。

二年級快結束時，在四月的某個星期一早上，布魯斯小姐出現了。那一年，我真正的導師是布萊托太太，她說：「這是布魯斯小姐，正在讀大學，她在學習如何當一位老師。她

會來我們班上一陣子，那是她大學課業的一部分。」

我看著布魯斯小姐，她比布萊托太太年輕，年輕很多，年輕到看起來有點像是林克‧貝柯斯特的姊姊，只不過林克的姊姊才在念高中，外加有一部分的頭髮染成粉紅色，或者有時候是紫色。

布魯斯小姐的頭髮是金色帶一點淡紅色。看到她的第一天，她穿著藍色的襯衫、綠色的裙子和藍色的鞋子。她的鼻子有點小，或許是因為她戴了一副黑框大眼鏡，鼻子的大部分被眼鏡遮住了。她的鼻子上還有雀斑。

到班上前三天，布魯斯小姐沒有做多少事。她有時候幫布萊托太太發考卷；有一次大聲朗讀了一段故事。不過大部

分的時間，她都只是坐在教室後面的一張椅子上觀察。

到了星期三，我們已經很習慣她待在教室裡了。沒有人太去注意布魯斯小姐，除了我以外。我在一開始的那三天，一直在觀察她。

而我注意到一件事。

二年級那時候，威利和我都在布萊托太太班上，所以我在星期三的午餐時間問了威利一個問題。我問他：「你有注意到布魯斯小姐有什麼地方怪怪的嗎？」

「怪怪的地方？」威利說：「你是說，像是她看黑板時瞇著眼睛、皺著鼻子的樣子嗎？我覺得那樣有點好笑，你不覺得嗎？」

「不是啦，」我說：「我是說她奇怪的地方。你有看過她笑嗎？」

威利正在用他的前牙刮掉奧利奧餅乾的糖霜，他就停在餅乾正中間。他的眼睛睜得很大說：「你說得對！我從來沒看她笑過！你看過嗎？」

我搖搖頭。「沒，一次也沒有，不知道為什麼？」

威利刮完第一片餅乾，開始舔剩下的部分。他停下來的時候，舌頭還伸出來，然後他大口大口吞得超快，還說：

「嘿！說不定她**沒辦法**笑！說不定她有某種特別的毛病，比如說只要笑了，牙齒就會掉下來或什麼的！或者也許……也許她是……一個**外星人**！沒錯，她是外星人……她不知道怎麼

笑，而且⋯⋯而且她會運用她的特殊能力⋯⋯把我們統統變

成漢堡，然後把我們傳送到她的太空船去！」

威利就是那樣，他很有想像力。

可是就某方面來說，威利是對的，布魯斯小姐**的確好像**

有某些特殊的能力。

她擁有的其中一種能力即將暫時改變我的人生，因為布

魯斯小姐就快要把我變成班上的小丑，傑克・德瑞克。

2 嚇呆了

星期四早上，布萊托太太要我們全部安靜注意聽。她要布魯斯小姐過來站在她旁邊，就在教室的前方。然後布萊托太太說：「接下來幾個星期，布魯斯小姐會當你們的老師。這段時間我會在圖書館幫李德太太的忙，所以我可能每天還是看得到你們，甚至有時候會進教室。不過布魯斯小姐會是你們的老師，我希望你們都能為她做出最棒的表現。」

接著，布萊托太太就拿起她的皮包和一疊文件走出教室。

我們全都坐在位子上看著布魯斯小姐。布魯斯小姐站在教室前面看著我們。她說：「我們先講好規矩。」她的聲音聽起來有點高又尖銳。「首先，我的教室必須非常安靜。不准聊天，不准竊竊私語，也不准大吼大叫或大笑。只有先舉手並得到我的同意，才准講話。我們有很多工作要做，沒有時間摸魚。我對你們每個人的期望都很高，我要求完美的表現。

這樣清楚嗎？」

布魯斯小姐抬高眉毛，把眉毛撐到她的大眼鏡上方，然後環視全班。她沒有笑。

我也看看四周，看到每個人臉上那種神情，是害怕的模

樣，就連林克‧貝柯斯特看起來都很害怕，這種狀況幾乎從來不曾發生過。

布魯斯小姐雙手拍了兩下，然後說：「好了。現在我們別再浪費時間，請拿出你們的數學作業本。」

蘿拉‧培爾舉起手，布魯斯小姐向她點點頭。蘿拉說：「我們都是先閱讀，再作數學。」

布魯斯小姐沒有笑。她說：「你叫什麼名字？」

「蘿拉。」

布魯斯小姐說：「蘿拉，我要你來回答我一個問題，可以嗎？」

蘿拉真的非常小聲的說：「可以。」

「蘿拉，現在，」布魯斯小姐說：「誰是你的老師？」

蘿拉微笑了，因為那個問題很簡單。她說：「我的老師是布萊托太太。」

布魯斯小姐揚起眉毛，身體向前傾，她說：「嗯，蘿拉，請想清楚，布萊托太太剛才說過什麼？你們接下來幾個星期的老師是誰？」

蘿拉用微弱的小小聲音說：「是你。」

布魯斯小姐對她點點頭，說：「你說得對，蘿拉，現在**我**是你的老師。一分鐘前，我要你們做什麼？」

蘿拉說：「你叫我們拿出數學作業本。」

布魯斯小姐點點頭。「現在，我再說一次。同學們，請拿

出你們的數學作業本。」

所以我們照做了。我們全都拿出數學作業本，照布魯斯小姐說的那樣翻到四十七頁，然後做了一些加法習題。沒有人說話，沒有人竊竊私語，沒有人看窗外，也沒有人笑。

布魯斯小姐一下指令，我們就從作業本裡撕下練習紙。

布魯斯小姐一下指令，我們就把名字寫在紙上，然後我們把練習紙往前傳。安安靜靜。

接下來是社會課。我們得閱讀三頁《人群與地方》這本書。安安靜靜。然後回答八十三頁上的一些問題。我們不能交談，也不能看隔壁同學寫什麼，只能寫下自己的答案。布魯斯小姐是這樣說的，她好像認為我們會作弊的樣子。而且

她沒有笑。

我看著蘿拉・培爾。她的臉沒有動，有點像是戴著一張面具。她直挺挺的坐在位置上，一點笑容都沒有，眼睛始終朝下盯著桌子。她把工作完成後，就雙手交疊放在膝蓋上。

她看起來像一座雕像。

我知道蘿拉為什麼會那個樣子，她怕犯錯，布魯斯小姐嚇到她了——嚇到呆掉了。因為當你遇到的老闆是個生氣鬼時，就可能會發生這種狀況。假如你的老闆愛生氣、吹毛求疵又愛挑剔，情況又特別嚇人。

我們的教室安靜極了，只能聽見布魯斯小姐的藍色鞋子在教室裡走來走去時發出的吱吱聲。

我很快看了一下其他小孩。威利很害怕，安德莉亞・塞爾頓也是。每個人都嚇呆了，就連比林克・貝柯斯特還不容易被嚇到的班・葛朗森也一樣。

我也是。我坐著不動，威利和我坐在同一組，只隔了六十公分遠，可是我完全沒在看他，因為我怕我們會對彼此微笑，然後被當場抓到，那樣布魯斯小姐可能會對我們發飆。

一部分的我決定要小心行事，一部分的我想要確定自己不會惹上任何麻煩。

可是還有另外一部分的我，並不想要像一袋馬鈴薯那樣坐在那裡；這部分的我不想要只是雙手交疊、眼睛朝下看著我的桌子。

有一部分的我不在乎布魯斯小姐有沒有發飆，那個部分的我想要倒立、吐舌頭，然後大喊，喊得很大聲。

可是我有這樣嗎？

沒有。那是布魯斯小姐接手我們班的第一天，我不敢。

就跟所有其他人一樣，我太害怕了。

3 嚇傻了

星期五早上我通常都很開心。

星期五表示隔天就是星期六，而大部分的星期六，威利和我都會一起閒晃。我們會看看電視、騎騎腳踏車、玩一些電腦遊戲，通常就是在玩耍。如果天氣好的話，我們就會在威利家後面的樹林裡加強我們的堡壘。所以星期五就表示那個星期的工作幾乎做完了。

可是布魯斯小姐接手後的那個星期五，我並不覺得開心，感覺上那將是我人生中最艱難的一天。

那天在搭公車去學校的路上，我心想：「說不定布魯斯小姐今天會比較親切一些，說不定她會稍微笑一下，今天的情況可能會比昨天好很多。」

我錯了。

星期五開始的方式就和星期四一樣。我們先做了一張數學學習單，不過我們並不是把學習單往前傳，而是互相交換。布魯斯小姐為我們唸出正確答案，而且她完全沒有笑。

之後我們在社會課做了一張訓練地圖技巧的作業。我們標出東、南、西、北，把河流和湖泊塗上藍色，找出鐵路和

公路、山脈和城市，接著布魯斯小姐把頭上的投影機打開，讓我們看看我們的地圖應該長成什麼樣子。她說如果我們的地圖有做錯任何地方，可以修改過來。她那樣做還算不錯，可是她從來不笑。

體育課很棒，不是因為我愛體育課，因為我大部分的時候都不愛，體育課很棒，是因為布魯斯小姐不在旁邊。

體育課以後，我們全都回到教室。沒有人笑、沒有人遲到，甚至連慢一秒鐘也沒有。

然後布魯斯小姐說我們要玩小蜜蜂拼字遊戲，每個人都很高興。小蜜蜂拼字遊戲總是很好玩，對吧？錯，布魯斯小姐是老闆的時候就一點也不好玩了。

布魯斯小姐低頭看看座位表，然後透過她的大眼鏡，看著梅根‧萊特。她說：「梅根，從你開始。記住我們的規則：你要先說出那個單字，然後把單字拼出來，接著再唸一次那個單字。準備好了嗎？」

梅根點點頭，於是布魯斯小姐說：「第一個字是『mouse』（老鼠）。」

梅根抬頭看著天花板，然後她做了一個深呼吸，說：「M-o-……」

布魯斯小姐搖搖頭說：「請停下來。」

梅根真的非常快的說：「噢，噢……我知道，我忘記先說出那個字了，對不對？Mouse；m-o-……」

嚇傻了

布魯斯小姐搖搖頭說：「我很抱歉，梅根，可是你沒有按照規則，我們都要學會完全依照指示來做，這非常重要。

所以這表示你**出局了**。」

梅根說：「可是有時候我們會有第二次機會，因為我會拼這個字。」

布魯斯小姐沒有笑，她甚至連眼睛都沒有眨一下。她搖搖頭說：「我堅信隨時保持思考非常重要，我那樣期許自己，也那樣期望你們每一個人。我很抱歉，可是你**出局了**。」

布魯斯小姐低頭看看座位表，但我繼續望著梅根。我為她感到難過，她正咬著下唇，看起來好像快哭了。

布魯斯小姐的眼光從座位表往上移，她直直看著威利

說：「菲利浦，題目是『mouse』。」

威利微笑著說：「嗯，布魯斯小姐？每個人都叫我威利，因為我姓『威利斯』，比起菲利浦，我也比較喜歡威利，所以你可以叫我威利。」

布魯斯小姐看著威利說：「等我們彼此更熟一點的時候，我可能就會叫你的小名，可是現在，我想要叫你的本名，好嗎？現在，菲利浦，第一個字是『mouse』。」

有一秒鐘的時間，威利看起來好像以為布魯斯小姐叫他菲利浦是在開玩笑，但她只是揚起眉毛站在那裡等著，接著威利就知道她是說真的。

威利驚訝到不知道該怎麼辦，所以他就用力吞了一兩次

口水，接著又吞了更多次。

布魯斯小姐說：「我猜菲利浦還沒有準備好要玩，所以這一輪菲利浦**出局**了。」她又再一次向下看著座位表，接著就直直看著我。「傑克，第一個字是『mouse』。」

也許是梅根臉上的表情，也許是威利坐在那邊猛吞口水的模樣，或者是布魯斯小姐不斷的說「出局」的方式，我不知道到底是什麼，可是我的腦袋裡有個東西突然發出劈啪聲。

我直直的看著布魯斯小姐，然後用一種又高又尖銳的聲音說：「Mouse: m-i-c-k-e-y; mouse ❶。」

❶ 傑克在這裡故意將 mouse 拼成 Mickey（米奇），也就是迪士尼卡通明星米老鼠的名字。

41

每個人都花了幾秒鐘才想到我剛才拼了什麼字，接下來，教室裡的每個小孩聽起來好像都深深吸了一口氣，然後屏住呼吸。

布魯斯小姐從她的大眼鏡裡瞪著我。「那個字**沒講對**！」

所以我就繼續用我最棒的米老鼠聲音說：「嘻嘻——好吧，我猜我**出局了**。」

我也猜到自己麻煩大了，可是一部分的我並不在乎。

布魯斯小姐的臉脹得通紅，她手裡的紙開始搖晃，她看起來就像一隻準備跳起來的貓。

然後布魯斯小姐走近我的椅子三步。她皺著眉頭說：「傑克，那並**不好笑**！」

我很快的環顧教室一眼，每個人都露齒而笑，威利幾乎就快受不了了。

布魯斯小姐錯了。**是**很好笑。非常好笑。

布魯斯小姐有開始對我大叫嗎？她有叫我直接到校長辦公室去嗎？她有沒有說：「傑克・德瑞克，**你**放學之後過來找我！」？

沒有。

布魯斯小姐低頭看著那張座位表。她持續看了大概有五秒鐘，那是我生命中最漫長的五秒鐘。從頭到尾，我都一直看著她的臉。

然後布魯斯小姐抬頭往上看，並且說：「安妮，題目還

43

是『mouse』。拼出來，拜託——**請拼對。**」

安妮拼完字後，布魯斯小姐只是繼續進行小蜜蜂拼字的遊戲。**她表現得就像剛剛沒有發生任何事！**

可是剛才有事發生。事實上，有兩件事發生。

第一件事是，我在全班同學面前做了一件傻事：每個人幾乎都快要爆出大笑，他們覺得我真的很好笑！以前從來沒有發生過這種事，我還滿喜歡這樣的。此外，我並沒有惹上麻煩。太神奇了！

剛才發生的第二件事就比較像是個謎了，因為我不是真的很確定它有沒有發生，而那件事就發生（應該說是，**可能發生**）在布魯斯小姐低頭看著座位表的時候，就在我看著她

嚇傻了

的臉的時候。謎題就是：我覺得我看到了某個東西。

某個我之前從來沒看過的東西。

就在布魯斯小姐臉上，只有短短一秒鐘。

而那看起來有點像是⋯⋯一個**微笑**。

4 祕密消息

到了星期一的圖書館時間，我已經確定我星期五看到的東西是弄錯了。布魯斯小姐的微笑？就算是一個小小的迷你微笑？絕不可能。

整個星期一早上我們都很努力工作。布魯斯小姐不斷逼迫我們，一秒鐘也不放過。數學作業、地圖技能、書本閱讀、拼字訓練，就連早上的休息時間都不好玩了，因為我們

知道後面還有更多工作等著，更多工作，沒一點笑容。

不過，就在午餐時間以前，我們去了圖書館。圖書館時間很棒，有一整個小時的時間，還有成堆的書，而且沒有布魯斯小姐。我的意思是，她是在那裡沒錯，不過她得讓我們自己獨處一段時間。

我們一到那裡的時候，我對布萊托太太揮手，因為她正在圖書館裡幫忙。她對我微笑，也揮揮手。

然後我就去找我的羅賓漢故事書了。

《羅賓漢》是我從二年級開始最愛的書，我從來沒有把它借出去過，因為那樣一來我很可能只要兩天就看完了。我只在圖書館時間看這本書，那樣子會讓這本書看比較久，就像

好吃的硬彈珠糖可以吃很久一樣。

我馬上就知道該到哪裡找書，書果然在那裡。

所有的軟椅子都有人坐了，加上媒體中心前面有點吵，所以我就把我的書拿到大教室後面，那裡很安靜。

我坐在一些書架間的地毯上，靠著牆壁，然後翻開書，一下子就置身其中。我、羅賓漢與小約翰，騎著我們的馬穿過雪伍德森林。

我正看得入神的時候，聽見有人說：「我必須和你談一談。」一聲音並不是來自我的書，是圖書館裡的聲音。

我認得那個聲音，是布魯斯小姐。

我心想：**太棒了，我正看到書裡最精采的部分呢，她居**

然要跟我談話。

我站了起來，又聽見另一個聲音說：「好的，漢娜，我們就在這裡談談。」

我也認得那個聲音，是布萊托太太，就在書架另一端，距離我約九十公分。

我猜我大可以發出一點噪音，或是站起來看看書架上的書，這樣她們就會看到我。

可是我沒有，我覺得我可能會因為待在圖書館後面惹上麻煩，她們說不定都會對我大吼大叫。

所以我僵住了，就只是坐在那裡。

我試著不要聽，甚至把手蓋在耳朵上，但還是聽得見她

們的聲音。

布萊托太太說：「很抱歉我星期五下午沒有時間和你談。一切都還好嗎？」

布魯斯小姐說：「這個嘛，星期五的午餐時間前發生了一件事……我不確定該怎麼處理。」

「喔？」布萊托太太說：「發生什麼事？」

布魯斯小姐在說什麼？她說的是我，她告訴布萊托太太

我在進行小蜜蜂拼字遊戲時開的大玩笑。

我坐在那裡，不敢相信自己的耳朵。你知道光是聽到某人的聲音就能知道許多事嗎？嗯……就算沒有看到她，我可以感覺到布魯斯小姐正在微笑。微笑耶！

她甚至還咯咯笑了一下說：「真希望你有看到傑克的臉，他實在太有趣了！他真是可愛，我差點就要破功了！」

布萊托太太說：「嗯，幸好你沒有，一旦你開始跟著孩子們一起笑，事情可能很快就會失控。」

「我的大學老師也是這樣說，」布魯斯小姐說：「她跟我們說，原則就是『在聖誕節以前都不要笑。』」

布萊托太太輕聲笑著說：「對呀，我以前也有學到，那是個好原則，尤其是你才剛入行，或是對代課老師來說也一樣。有時候，只需要一個笑臉，小孩們就會以為他們要怎樣都行。」

她們安靜了幾秒鐘，接著布魯斯小姐說：「你認為呢？

我應該對傑克做什麼處理嗎？」

「傑克？」布萊托太太說：「別擔心，他是個好孩子，不過你還是得盯著他，如果那是你最大的問題，那麼聽起來你表現得不錯。現在我們最好回到前面，到孩子們的身邊去，他們開始有一點吵了。」

然後她們一面走遠，聲音變得愈愈小。

我就那樣坐在地板上。我的心臟怦怦跳，嘴巴很乾。

我向前爬，用眼睛偷瞄著書架一角。當沒有人在看的時候，我溜了出去，移到圖書館另一個角落去。

我感覺自己像是一個二年級的間諜。現在我掌握了一些祕密消息：布魯斯小姐不是外星人，她知道要怎麼微笑，還

祕密消息

有咯咯笑。

再加上，她覺得我很可愛。

最棒的是，她覺得我很**有趣**。

當你只有八歲，又得到這種祕密消息時，可能會引起某件事。

那件事就叫做麻煩。

勢不可擋

5 勢不可擋

星期一整個午餐時間，我都想告訴威利。我想告訴他布魯斯小姐會咯咯笑，還有我很可愛的事。

可是我沒有，因為祕密最棒的部分在於它成為祕密的原因，就是不能洩漏出去。

午休後回到教室，我不確定自己該怎麼做。所以有一會兒的時間，除了更多作業以外，我沒有做任何事，因為午餐

後我們馬上又有默讀時間。

布魯斯小姐叫我們看閱讀課本裡的一個故事，已經看完故事的人就接著讀第二個故事，讀完第二個故事的人就讀第三個故事。這樣一來，閱讀速度快的人就有事可忙，閱讀速度慢的人也可以把第一則故事看完。

然後，等所有人都讀完第一個故事以後，我們就要來討論這個故事。

我二年級的時候閱讀的速度就已經很快，所以在我幾乎要看完第三個故事時，布魯斯小姐拍了兩下手說：「好了，全班同學們，請每個人把閱讀課本翻到七十七頁，我們開始來討論這個故事裡有誰。」。布魯斯小姐往下看著座位表說：

「安琪亞，你可以告訴我們故事裡一個角色的名字嗎？」

安琪亞照做了。她說：「吉姆。」

這不是很難，整個故事裡只出現了三個人，而且故事只有十二頁，又有很多圖片。

由卡洛斯回答了下一個「誰」，而莉莎回答了最後一個「誰」。

我們完成了「誰」的部分，這實在很無聊，我覺得布萊托太太會做得好一點。

可是這就是布魯斯小姐會在這裡的原因，這樣子她才可以學會變得比較不無聊，也許是在將來的某一天。

答完「誰」之後，就是「在哪裡」。

布魯斯小姐說：「現在，告訴全班同學故事發生在哪裡，林克。」

這也超簡單。

只不過林克並沒有在聽。

林克把某個東西推到桌子下面，看著布魯斯小姐。他的眼睛裡有那種神情——失落的神情。

林克說：「嗯……哪裡？喔，對喔……哪裡。嗯……問題是什麼？」

布魯斯小姐把頭歪向一邊，向下看著林克在桌子底下的手，然後她的眼睛微瞇、嘴唇緊閉。

我知道接下來會發生什麼事，我全部都看得到：布魯斯

小姐會走過來伸出手，然後她會說：「林克，把那個東西給我。」林克會拉出一本漫畫書或玩具，或是什麼蠢東西。布魯斯小姐會瞪著他看，直到他真的覺得很害怕為止。她會讓林克後悔自己沒有專心，就像她對蘿拉和梅根做的一樣。

二年級那時候，林克人不太善良，他大部分時間都是個霸凌者，所以我不是很常為林克感到難過。

可是那次不一樣。在那當下，我為他感到難過。我對布魯斯小姐感到有點生氣，因為我覺得她也像是某種霸凌者。

所以在布魯斯小姐有機會走向林克以前，我舉起手，並且開始揮舞。

布魯斯小姐轉過來看著我。

她不想理會我，我看得出她還沒有處理完林克的事，不過我還是一直不斷在空中揮舞著我的手。

所以布魯斯小姐說：「傑克，怎麼了？」她不用看座位表就知道我的名字。

我說：「我想我知道故事發生在哪裡。」

布魯斯小姐不確定該怎麼做。她想要管林克，可是她現在已經叫了我，而我有答案。所以她說：「好吧，那麼……傑克，告訴我們。在哪裡？」

「這個嘛……」我慢慢的說：「我不是**非常**確定……」

她很快的說：「那麼只要告訴我們你**覺得**故事發生在哪裡就好了，傑克。」布魯斯小姐只想趕快結束我這部分，好回

勢不可擋

去處理林克。

我說：「所以我應該直接告訴你嗎？現在就告訴你？」

她對我點點頭。

我用更慢的速度說：「就算我不是**完完全全確定**？」

布魯斯小姐說：「是的，傑克，就算只是猜測。你覺得

這個故事發生在**哪裡**？」

我直直看著布魯斯小姐的眼睛說：「嗯，我……我**覺得**

故事發生在……地球上！」

我直直瞪著布魯斯小姐的眼睛看。我聽見我後面一個女

生咯咯的笑聲，可是我沒有笑，我試著連眼睛都不眨，只是

等待著。

教室裡每個小孩都知道我剛才開了一個玩笑。布魯斯小

姐也知道。可是我繼續裝成很嚴肅的樣子。

如果她還是覺得我很可愛，那表示布魯斯小姐掩飾得很

好。她把嘴唇抿成一條細線，氣沖沖的瞪著我。然後她說：

「對，沒錯，傑克，故事**當然**發生在地球上。」她沒有笑，連

一絲絲都沒有。

她轉回去面向林克。現在林克舉手了。不管他之前把什

麼東西藏在桌子底下，現在已經消失了。

布魯斯小姐對他點點頭。林克說：「故事發生在海邊，

對吧？」

「對，林克。」布魯斯小姐說。然後她做了一個深呼吸。

我以為她準備走向林克，不管三七二十一的對他發脾氣，或是說不定她會轉過來，對我發飆。

可是她沒有，她吐出深呼吸的那口氣，然後又向下看著她的座位表。她說：「現在，泰德，你可以告訴我故事裡發生了**什麼事**嗎？」

泰德很痛苦，他的嘴角扭動著，他想要微笑，可是他知道他最好不要。

我環顧教室。教室裡有一半的小孩正在微笑，另一半就像泰德那樣試著不要笑出來。

整間教室裡只有一個人沒有感覺到任何樂趣，那個人就是布魯斯小姐。

然而我不是在想著布魯斯小姐的事，那個時候沒有。我太忙了，我在享受我自己，因為這是兩天以來的第二次，我做了有趣的事，而且我兩次都逃過了處罰！

我是班上新的小丑。我勢不可擋。

6 搞笑先生

星期一下午放學回到家時，我問媽媽可不可以吃點心，因為這麼搞笑害我肚子好餓。

所以媽媽幫我做了些花生醬夾心餅乾，外加一杯牛奶。

我一邊吃，一邊開始想。我試著回想我之前曾經在學校表現有趣的時候，像是我還在一年級或是幼稚園時。我試著回想，卻想不起任何一次。

現在，我突如其來的讓每個人都開始想笑，還成功兩次

耶！居然這麼容易，我甚至沒有太認真就成功了。

我的牛奶才喝到一半就停了下來。我在心裡對自己說：

「如果你根本沒有太認真就這麼好笑了，想想看，如果你真的

努力搞笑會有多好笑！」我確定自己可能會成為全宇宙有史

以來最好笑的小孩！而且我可以第二天就開始！

如果我要變得超級好笑，就會需要超級笑話，而且我要

講這些笑話講得恰到好處。

所以我去找艾比，她是我妹妹。我念二年級的時候，艾

比在上幼稚園。我發現她在房間裡聽《三隻小豬》的卡帶。

我過去把錄放音機關掉。

艾比說：「嘿！我還要聽耶！」

「等一下啦，」我說：「因為我想試試講笑話給你聽，可以嗎？」

艾比雙手交叉在胸前，皺起眉頭。「我不想聽笑話，我要聽小豬。」

「拜託嘛，」我說：「會很好笑啦。你準備好了嗎？」

艾比抓抓她的膝蓋，然後對天花板扮了一個鬼臉。她在她床邊坐起身，然後說：「好了。」

我說：「敲敲門。」

艾比皺皺鼻子說：「什麼？」

「我說：『敲敲門。』你知道的呀。這是敲敲門笑話。」

艾比搖搖頭。「那又不好笑。」

「那是因為笑話還沒講完啦。聽好，」我說：「敲門。」

「敲門。」然後你就說：『是誰呀？』好嗎？」接著我說：「敲門。」

艾比說：「是誰呀？好嗎？」

「不對啦，」我說：「你只要說：『是誰呀？』講那樣就好了。只有『是誰呀？』就好，現在我們再試一次吧。準備好了嗎？」

艾比點點頭。

所以我說：「敲敲門。」

艾比說：「是誰呀？」

我說：「土豆。」

艾比笑了。她拍拍手說：「土豆很好笑耶，再講另一個笑話吧。」

「不對啦，不對啦，」我說：「『土豆』還不是最好笑的部分。我說：『敲敲門。』你說：『是誰呀？』然後我說：『土豆。』你再說：『吐誰呀？』**那時候我才結束笑話。❷**

艾比看著我。她說：「土豆**就**很好笑了，我才不要別的笑話。」

❷ 這個笑話在「是誰呀？」之後的「土豆。」原文是「Toodle.」因為 toodle 有「再見」的意思，所以接下來原文用 "Toodle who?" "Bye-bye." 這類的對話來呈現笑點。中文在此只能改以音譯來取代原文在音義上的諧趣。

「拜託啦，」我說：「我必須把笑話講完，可以嗎？我要再重新講一次。」

艾比皺著眉頭。「才不要咧。」

可是我還是說：「敲敲門。」

艾比說：「是誰呀？好嗎？」

「不對！」我大叫。「你只要說『是誰呀？』就好了。艾比，把話說對！」

艾比搖搖頭，然後大叫：「**媽咪──媽咪──！**」艾比真的很會叫。

媽媽大概兩秒鐘就跑上樓，進到艾比的房間。「怎麼了？」然後媽看到我了。她說：「喔！傑克，很好，你受傷了嗎？」

你也在這裡。你們都還好吧？艾比，你怎麼那樣叫我？」

艾比指著我。「因為他啦，他不肯停止講笑話。」

媽對我皺眉。「傑克，你又在開艾比的玩笑了嗎？」

「才不是！」我說：「我沒有在開她玩笑。我只不過在試著講一個愚蠢的敲敲門短笑話而已。她連回答都不會，我快被她逼瘋了！」

媽媽說：「好啦，你為什麼不試講那個敲敲門笑話給我聽呢？這樣艾比就能在旁邊聽，看效果怎麼樣，如何？」

我說：「好吧。敲敲門。」

媽說：「是誰呀？」

我說：「土豆。」

笑話。

我站在五斗櫃上的鏡子前面。我看看自己，然後開始講

那時候我就進房去，練習自己講笑話。

艾比搖頭。「不好笑，只要說土豆就好，土豆比較好笑。」

媽微笑著點頭。她說：「這個笑話不錯。」

我說：「土豆吐一吐！」

媽說：「吐誰呀？」

敲敲門。

是誰呀？

七、八、九。

搞笑先生

七、八、九是誰呀？

奇奇扒了九片餅乾！

敲敲門。

是誰呀？

知更鳥來了。

知更鳥呼呼叫嗎？

不！知更鳥啾啾叫；貓頭鷹才呼呼叫！

誰有「笑到發瘋症」？

一個把自己的頭笑掉的男人！

如果我一隻手有五顆棒球，

另一隻手也有五顆棒球，

我會得到什麼？

真的超大的手！❸

比在你的蘋果裡找到一條蟲更糟的是什麼？

找到半條蟲！

講笑話給自己聽不太有趣，所以我很快就覺得累了。可

是我看著鏡子裡的自己時，才想起我有多會扮鬼臉。

我練習鬥雞眼、吐舌頭。我練習把鼻頭往上推，做出小豬臉。我練習鼓起臉頰，還把眼皮拉成怪樣子。毫無疑問的，我是一個很好笑的小孩。

但是才過了一會兒，我的臉就覺得累了。我的眼睛因為鬥雞眼做太久，開始覺得痛。

我在書櫃上搜尋，直到找到一本在書展買的笑話集。我坐在床上看完整本書，然後又趴下來，把笑話集再看一次，從頭到尾一整本。

我猜是搞笑讓我很累，因為我把臉埋在笑話集裡睡著

❸「超大的手」原文 BIG hands，也有「熱情掌聲」的意思。

了。我醒來時，發現媽媽正在叫我下樓吃晚餐。

我走進廚房的時候，爸爸對著我微笑說：「嘿，傑克！

有什麼新的玩意嗎？」

我說：「月亮。」

爸爸說：「月亮？」

我說：「對呀。每個月都有新月啊。」

爸和媽笑了。爸說：「很好笑唷，傑克。」

艾比說：「才沒有土豆好笑。」

我們全都坐在餐桌前，我望著食物。我馬上就說：「嘿，

媽，你知道他們都把懶惰的牛做成什麼嗎？鹹（閒）牛肉！

懂了嗎？『遊手好閒』的『閒』和『鹹死人』的『鹹』同音？

那是我剛剛編的耶！很好笑，對吧？」

媽媽微笑著點點頭，一面傳給我們馬鈴薯。「對，很好笑，傑克。」

我說：「嘿，爸，你知道農夫為什麼要把蒸汽機開過他的田地嗎？」

爸笑了起來，搖搖他的頭。我說：「因為他要種一些馬鈴薯泥！」

爸笑著說：「馬鈴薯泥！這個好笑！」

整個晚餐時間笑話不斷出現，像是我看見的所有東西都被變成笑話了。有時候是我想起看過的笑話，有時候是我亂編的。我甚至在艾比喝牛奶的時候做出我的搞笑魚臉，搞得

一團亂，可是那樣也超好笑！

我們吃點心的時候，我說：「嘿，爸，你吃冰淇淋的時候是用右手吃，還是用左手吃？」

「我想我是用右手吃。」

我說：「那就好笑啦……我都是用**湯匙吃**！」

我讓人笑破肚皮！

我要離席的時候，爸說：「你今晚真的是搞笑先生耶，傑克。這一切是怎麼開始的呢？」

我像個蠢蛋似的回答：「喔，是從學校開始的。」

講錯話了。

爸立刻皺起眉頭。他說：「這個嘛，我希望你在明天早

上以前把這些事忘光光。在學校這樣搞笑不是個好主意，傑克。你了解吧，可以嗎？」

我點點頭說：「喔，我知道。」那是真的，我知道那樣不是個好主意。

不，星期二在學校搞笑不是個**好**主意，那是個超級**棒**的主意！

7 四月的聖誕節

星期二早上，布魯斯小姐準備了堆積如山的工作，我為了要當搞笑先生做的練習沒有派上任何用場。我們的功課多到根本沒有機會講半個笑話。

再加上布魯斯小姐表現得愈來愈火大。

我們在做數學作業的時候，卡洛斯站了起來，開始走到教室後面。

布魯斯小姐看著他說：「卡洛斯，請待在你的座位上繼續寫作業，數學課就要結束了。」

他舉起鉛筆。「我得削這枝筆。」

布魯斯小姐說：「我確定這枝鉛筆夠你現在用，請繼續寫作業。」

卡洛斯說：「可是我作數學的時候，鉛筆必須非常尖，這樣我才能把數字寫得很漂亮。」

布魯斯小姐說：「我剛才叫你做什麼？卡洛斯？」

卡洛斯說：「你叫我坐下，可是我是說真的，我必須把鉛筆削尖一點。」

布魯斯小姐說：「卡洛斯，你在浪費時間，你得把所有

的數學習題都做完。所以坐下，回去寫作業，現在。」

卡洛斯慢慢走回他的位置坐了下來。

安妮立刻越過桌子，遞給卡洛斯一枝鉛筆。

布魯斯小姐盯著安妮說：「安妮！你在做**什麼**？」

安妮呆掉了，沒辦法回話。

布魯斯小姐說：「安妮，回答我！」

於是安妮聳聳肩膀，然後回答：「我有多一枝鉛筆，一枝削得很尖的鉛筆。」

布魯斯小姐皺著眉頭。我還以為她準備要大吼了，可是她說：「很好，安妮，你真貼心。現在，你們兩個人都回來寫作業，因為沒有完成數學習題的人，下課的時間都得待在

教室裡。」

　　布魯斯小姐表現得這麼生氣，讓我又覺得有點害怕了。就像我爸爸說過，嘗試在學校搞笑似乎不是個好主意。我想講笑話，但是可不想讓火車追著跑。在那個當下，布魯斯小姐似乎很像是火車頭。

　　所以我就把我的數學習題作完，其他每一個人也是。接著布魯斯小姐叫我們拿出拼字作業簿，我們照做了。然後布魯斯小姐叫我們翻到第六十二頁，我們也照做了，然後我們就立刻開始工作。

　　拼字作業很簡單，這種功課讓你的腦袋還有很多空間想其他的事情，所以我就開始想著自己前一天晚上在晚餐時有

多麼好笑。

坐在那裡抄寫用 tch 結尾的單字時，我想到一件在家忘記練習的事，一件很好笑的事。那件事我非常拿手，就是：製造噪音。

像是用嘴巴發出劈啪響的聲音。我可以把舌頭從口腔的上顎往外拉，發出超大的「啵」聲。這是很棒的音響。

我還會作出很棒的鴨子音效，我可以把嘴巴其中一側的空氣擠出來，發出呱呱聲，再加上我會像唐老鴨那樣笑。

不過我最厲害的音效是我和威利到對方家過夜時常常練習的聲音，就是打嗝。威利也很會打嗝，只是我更厲害。

要製造出很大的打嗝聲，你需要做的就是把一些空氣大

口吞進肚子裡，然後再把空氣嗝出來。簡單。

所以那個星期二早上，我坐在那裡做我的拼字作業，另外一邊想著打嗝的事。

我寫下 patch（補丁），然後吞了一口空氣。

我寫下 catch（抓住），吞了一口空氣。

我寫下 latch（門閂），吞一口空氣。

我寫下 pitch（柏油），再吞一口空氣。

我寫下 ditch（水溝），又多吞一口空氣。

我一直到吞下第五口空氣時才想起一件事。我不是在威利家過夜，我在學校。

我在椅子上坐直身子，稍微往後靠一點點。感覺就像我

的Ｔ恤底下塞了一顆氣球，可是那不是氣球，是我的肚子。

我用鉛筆敲敲肚子，發出一種中空的聲音，一種咚咚聲。

布魯斯小姐就在那時突然出現在我背後說：「傑克，你

所有的題目都做完了嗎？」

我用超快的速度轉過身，向上看著她的臉說：「沒有。」

我是**試著**要那樣說，可是，我**實際上**說出來的話卻是：

「沒………有。」

那是我這輩子以來最長、最大聲的嗝！

教室裡完全沒有聲音，每個人都瞪著我看，包括布魯斯

小姐。

別問我怎麼會有下一件事的主意，因為我不知道。布魯

我是傑克，天才搞笑王

斯小姐交叉著手臂，透過她巨大的黑色眼鏡往下看著我，而那個時候我做了什麼？我輕拍著胸口，裝出鬥雞眼說：「不好意思！一定是因為我早餐吃了那隻青蛙的關係！」

布魯斯小姐站在那兒，她正試著要發火，她想要皺起眉頭，大吼大叫，對我揮舞她的手指，告訴我說我真是超級超級沒禮貌。

可是她沒辦法。我實在太好笑了，再加上我很可愛。

所以布魯斯小姐做了什麼？她笑了！而且那不是一個小小的微笑，是一個露出牙齒和整張嘴的超級大微笑，幾乎是咧嘴笑了。教室裡每個小孩都看到了那個微笑，而且他們還聽見她咯咯咯笑。

90

布魯斯小姐的大學老師曾經說過：「到聖誕節才能笑。」

那個四月的早晨，我就是聖誕老人。聖誕節來囉！

在布魯斯小姐微笑又咯咯笑以後，每個人都笑了，接著布魯斯小姐用手遮住她的嘴巴，然後搖搖頭，她試著要再擺出嚴肅的樣子。

她說：「我們都別做蠢事了，請繼續完成你們的拼字作業。」那樣滿有效的，我們全部開始安靜下來。

接著威利發出幾乎和我一樣大的打嗝聲，說：「我早餐吃了兩隻青蛙唷！」

所有的小孩都因為他這句話笑了，笑得比剛才更大聲。

蘇珊・塔托說：「噢！噁心！」

當一個班級開始笑的時候，有點像是一座火山開始發出隆隆聲。因為一開始好像沒什麼，可是還是很危險。

布魯斯小姐拍手拍了兩次說：「同學們，夠囉！」

可是全班同學不覺得這樣夠了，我們才剛剛開始呢。

林克·貝柯斯特站了起來，把他的手夾在手臂下，開始在教室後面跳過來、跳過去。「嘿，快看！看呀！我是青蛙，呱呱！呱呱！」

布魯斯小姐又拍拍手。「林克，坐下！所有人，安靜！」

沒有人在聽她說話。威利還在打嗝，林克還在教室後面跳來跳去。

然後，泰德對班扔了一個紙球，班又把球扔回來。卡洛

斯揮著手臂大喊：「嘿，泰德！泰德！扔過來！」

他們開始玩起抓球遊戲，安妮和梅根大叫：「耶！班！耶，卡洛斯！嘿，也把球丟過來給我們嘛！」

布魯斯小姐大喊：「**安靜！**」

可是教室裡的聲音愈來愈大、愈來愈吵，我們教室已經變成一座噴發著歡笑、喊叫與玩笑聲的火山。

一旦那種火山開始活動，通常只剩下一個東西可以阻止它，就是一位真正的老師。

此外，還有另一種方式可以平息火山，我那天早上就看到了那種狀況。

因為如果一位實習老師踮著腳並尖叫說：「停下來！停

下來！」然後放聲大哭，跑出教室，還把門甩上，火山就會停止爆發，而且教室會變得很安靜。

非常、非常安靜。

95

8 布萊托法官

布萊托太太在布魯斯小姐奪門而出的兩分鐘後走進教室。

二十三個小孩正在作拼字作業。

靜悄悄的。

甚至沒人抬頭看布萊托太太，沒有人敢。

布萊托太太坐在教室前面，她用一枝鉛筆敲著她的桌子說：「請停止寫你們的作業。」

我們全部都看著她的時候，她說：「現在，誰要告訴我布魯斯小姐上課的時候這裡發生什麼事？」

布萊托太太穿著白襯衫和黑毛衣，她看起來就像那些電視節目上的女法官——布萊托法官。她再度用鉛筆敲敲桌子，然後環視著教室。她說：「我在等喔……」

我想要站起來說：「法官大人，都是我的錯，我太好笑了，我還知道布魯斯小姐會偷偷咯咯笑，我不是有意打嗝的，可是打了嗝以後，我講了那些有關青蛙的話，那就是為什麼事情會變得那麼瘋狂。我真抱歉我那麼爆笑。」

可是我沒有那樣說。我什麼都沒說。

瑪莎‧麥考反而舉了手。布萊托太太叫她的時候，瑪莎

就開始講話。她還是以她平常那種提問的方式講話。她說：

「這個嘛，我們正在作我們的拼字作業對吧？因為你知道，今天是星期二吧？你知道布魯斯小姐怎樣嗎？在傑克打嗝以後，是她先開始笑的，你知道？嗯，你知道有時候要停下來不笑有多難嗎？你不覺得可能就是這麼一回事嗎？大家只不過停不下來，一直笑個不停是嗎？」

瑪莎講了很多話，可是布萊托太太就只聽到其中幾個字。布萊托太太轉過來看著我說：「『在傑克打嗝以後？』瑪莎剛才是不是說了『在傑克打嗝以後』？傑克，再多跟我說一點那部分的事。」

我說：「我不是故意的，不過就是我，是我打嗝了，那

是個很大的嗝，我又說了一些搞笑的話。」

布萊托太太揚起眉毛。她說：「搞笑的話？」

我點點頭。「對，我覺得應該很好笑吧，我說一定是因為我早餐吃了那隻青蛙的關係。」

布萊托太太的嘴角抽動了一下，不過她沒有笑。她說：

「我了解了，然後發生了什麼事？」

「情況變得有點瘋狂，整個班，在布魯斯小姐笑了以後。因為她從來都沒有笑過，在那個時候之前，連一次也沒有過，然後她也笑出聲來了，接下來⋯⋯就變得很吵。事情就是這樣。」

我猜我大可以告訴布萊托太太，泰德和班是怎樣的丟東

布萊托法官

西，還有女生們是怎樣大叫，還有威利怎樣一直打嗝打個不停，還有林克一直跳來跳去。

可是我沒有說，因為我知道要不是我那麼搞笑，其他事都不會發生。都是我的錯。

我猜布萊托太太也是那樣想，因為她站起來說：「同學們，李德太太正要過來。她到的時候，我要你們都把拼字作業做完，然後就默念課本，**安靜**的閱讀。」

然後她就轉身看著我。她說：「傑克，站起來，跟我走。」

我們走出法庭的時候，布萊托法官沒有笑。

我也沒有。

101

9 別再扮小丑

我以為布萊托法官要帶我去坐牢，就是去校長辦公室。

所以，當她大步走過辦公室時，我很驚訝。結果，她停在一扇標示著「教師休息室」的門前。她打開門說：「進去，傑克。」

我從來沒有進過教師休息室。那裡很不錯，有一張大沙發，還有冰箱。沙發前面有一張小桌子，上面放著一些雜

誌。有一面牆上是一塊很大的公布欄，公布欄上有點亂。有一座大書櫃，甚至還有一台可口可樂的販賣機，這肯定是全校最棒的一間房了。

布魯斯小姐就坐在房間中央的大桌子前。旁邊有一盒面紙。她的鼻子紅紅的。

布魯斯小姐的大眼鏡就放在那盒面紙旁邊。布魯斯小姐沒戴眼鏡，看起來就像高中生，一個眼睛腫腫、鼻水直流的女生。

布萊托太太從布魯斯小姐對面幫我拉了張椅子，她沿著桌子走，坐在她的實習老師旁邊。

布萊托太太說：「傑克，你有話想跟布魯斯小姐說嗎？」

我很想說：「敲敲門。」因為布魯斯小姐看起來好像需要一個笑話打氣，可是我知道那不是好主意，所以我說了布萊托太太希望我說的話。我說：「我很抱歉在班上搞笑，我很抱歉我那麼搞笑，讓你笑了出來。」

布魯斯小姐抹了一下眼睛說：「沒關係，傑克，很抱歉我這麼沮喪，我並不想，也不應該這樣。可是事情都結束了，所以沒關係了。」

布萊托太太搖搖頭說：「事實上，布魯斯小姐，不是沒關係，傑克除了乖乖的把功課做完以外，不應該嘗試做任何其他事。對吧，傑克？」我點點頭。「如果你不小心發出沒禮貌的噪音，你只需要說：『抱歉，不好意思。』這樣你了解

105

嗎？」我又點點頭。布萊托太太瞇著眼睛看著我的臉。「傑克，你是不小心的，對吧？你打嗝的時候？」

我回看布萊托太太的眼睛。我很高興可以說實話，因為布萊托法官一定看得出我在說謊。我說：「對，我不是故意打嗝的。」

布萊托太太點點頭。「至少我很高興知道情況是這樣。可是這種蠢事必須停下來。現在就停止。你了解嗎？」

我點頭。「嗯嗯，別再做蠢事。」

布萊托太太說：「那好吧，布魯斯小姐，你還有什麼事想要補充嗎？」

布魯斯小姐搖頭。她看起來好一點了，可是我還是看得

出來她有哭過。她說：「沒有，沒有其他事了。」

布萊托太太說：「傑克，你呢？有什麼話要說嗎？」

這是那種我該懂得閉嘴的時刻之一，我應該搖搖頭，看起來很害怕的坐著就好，或者我應該小小聲回答：「沒有了，謝謝您。」然後把手放在膝蓋上。可是我沒有。

我直直看著布魯斯小姐說：「布魯斯小姐，在今天之前你為什麼從來不笑？是因為你的老師說的話嗎？有關於聖誕節的話？」

慘了。**超慘**！在我說那句話的那一秒鐘，就知道自己又做了一件蠢事。

布魯斯小姐的眼睛睜得好大，布萊托太太也是。她們兩

個人都看著我，然後看看彼此，然後又看著我。布萊托太太交叉起手臂。

我知道她們知道了，她們知道我聽見她們那天在圖書館裡的對話。

布魯斯小姐從她的椅子上坐直。就算沒有戴大眼鏡，她的眼睛還是很嚇人。她說：「什麼⋯⋯你這個小**間諜**！你在**監視我！**」我真慶幸她是坐在大桌子的另一側。

我吞下口水，用超快的速度說：「不，真的，我不是在監視！在圖書館的那一天嗎？我不是有意要聽你們說話，我不是故意的，我只是坐在那邊看我的《羅賓漢》，你剛好走到我這邊，我很怕我會因為坐在視聽室後面而惹上麻煩，結果

你們就開始講話了。你們就這樣開始講話耶！我試著不要聽，可是還是聽見你們的聲音了。我不是故意的，而且我沒有告訴任何人那件事。真的！還有，我很抱歉。」我來來回回的看著她們兩個人的臉。

我看得出她們相信我，可是我還是覺得布魯斯小姐好像準備跳過桌子來抓我。

換布萊托太太說話了。她說：「傑克，看起來你對於今天的事好像有很多需要感到抱歉的地方，不過我想布魯斯小姐和我了解當時的狀況。只要布魯斯小姐能夠接受你的道歉，那麼我也可以，我們就把這件事忘掉吧。好不好，布魯斯小姐？」

布魯斯小姐點頭，不過不是很情願的點頭。

「太好了，所以，」布萊托太太說，一面站了起來，「你們兩個都回班上去吧。」

布魯斯小姐在她的座位上稍微跳了一下。

「我？」她問：「你是說我還要回去？你班上嗎？今天？」

布萊托太太向下看著布魯斯小姐，然後微微笑。「什麼？你當然得回去，就是現在，你是老師耶。」

布魯斯小姐看起來一副好像有人剛剛叫她去墓園散步的樣子，還是在半夜，手邊沒有手電筒。她很害怕。

就在那個時候我懂了：她怕**我們**，怕我們這些小孩！她怕噪音、蠢事，還有瘋狂狀態！布魯斯小姐嚇壞了，而布萊

托太太沒有，因為布萊托太太是真正的老師。

布魯斯小姐咬著她的嘴唇，她看著布萊托太太說：「你不覺得你應該陪我去嗎？」

布萊托太太搖搖頭。「不，你不會有事的，全班同學都會等著看傑克發生了什麼事，傑克要表現出被痛罵一頓的樣子，從這一刻起，傑克也得要當一個完美的**天使**。你要走回那間教室，讓所有的男生女生們看看你只不過笑了一下，不代表他們就可以盡情撒野、為所欲為。」

布魯斯小姐說：「可是……可是我**哭了耶**，全部的小孩都看到我哭著衝出教室！我**沒辦法**回去。」

布萊托太太微笑著拍拍布魯斯小姐的手臂。「親愛的，別

擔心。每個人都了解哭這回事，尤其是小孩。當這種狀況發生的時候，你就把臉擦乾，然後繼續做任何你該做的事。**你**有一整班小孩要教呢。」

然後布萊托太太扶著布魯斯小姐的椅背，這樣布魯斯小姐就不得不站起來。

「好啦，」布萊托太太說：「現在你和傑克馬上趕過去吧，圖書館還需要李德太太。傑克，從現在起，關於你的消息我只要聽到好事，這樣夠清楚了嗎？」

我點點頭。

接著布魯斯小姐和我沿著穿堂走到教室。

我照布萊托太太說的做。我走進教室。我坐了下來。我沒看任何人。我沒有笑。我試著看起來像剛剛捱過這輩子最糟糕的十分鐘。我試著看起來像剛剛捱過這輩子最糟糕的十分鐘。我試著看起來很高興自己還活著。

事實證明布萊托太太說得沒錯。沒有半個小孩繼續搞笑，沒有半個小孩發出噪音或者沒有禮貌。

布魯斯小姐表現得很棒。在所有大吼大叫、哭泣和奪門而出後，她表現得像是整件事沒什麼大不了的。因為她那樣表現，所以就真的沒什麼，像是沒發生過任何事的樣子。

可是事情的確發生過，而且我有證據，因為我還是繼續搞笑。

只不過我從來不在教室裡搞笑，布魯斯小姐或者布萊托

113

太太在附近的時候也不會這樣。

所以我主要是為了威利搞笑。在上學前、下課時間、體育課的時候，還有星期六。只要我一有機會就會講笑話給威利聽，對他發出好笑的噪音，或扮鬼臉。有一天的午餐時間，我扮了一個小豬臉，害威利笑得太用力，用力到把一大塊奧利奧餅乾直接從鼻子裡噴出來！我太強了！

可是大約三個禮拜以後，威利開始瘋瘋癲癲，我的笑話也快用完了，所以有一天我就停了下來。我很高興我那麼做，因為隨時都要搞笑真的很難。把耍寶留到特殊場合好多了，像是外出過夜，或是搭乘遊覽車的時候。

布魯斯小姐剩下來的實習時間過得很快，最棒的是，她

別再扮小丑

不像從前那麼容易發火、那麼挑剔，或是吹毛求疵了，就像布魯斯小姐不必非得是那個樣子，因為她不害怕了。我想，假如你能夠大笑和咯咯笑，看著你的班級抓狂、尖叫又吼叫，接著大哭跑出教室，**然後**又回來讓所有事情都順利進行，那也沒有剩下多少事能讓你害怕了。

布萊托太太計畫了一個驚喜派對，在布魯斯小姐三週實習結束的最後時刻舉行。我們全班都在美術課為她做了一張大卡片，還都在上面簽名。當布萊托太太送她一本書並給她一個擁抱時，我還以為布魯斯小姐準備再一次大哭，然後跑出教室。

可是她沒有。她一直眨眼睛，然後笑了。是一個很大的

微笑，牙齒和全部東西都露出來的那種微笑。她的聲音聽起來有一點抖。她說：「我在戴普雷小學這裡學到好多。而且我知道，不論我去了多少地方，不論我教了多少其他的孩子，我永遠都不會忘記你們。」

布魯斯小姐是在對全班同學說話，可是到最後，她直直望著我。我感覺到她的意思是：她永遠也不會忘記我，傑克‧德瑞克，班上的小丑。